Also by LEE BENNETT HOPKINS

and Illustrated by Vera Rosenberry

A-HAUNTING WE WILL GO

Witching Time

Mischievous Stories and Poems Selected by
Lee Bennett Hopkins

and *Illustrated by* **Vera Rosenberry**

Albert Whitman & Company, Chicago

Acknowledgments

Every effort has been made to trace the ownership of all copyrighted
material and to secure the necessary permissions to reprint these
selections. In the event of any question arising as to the use of any
material, the editor and the publisher, while expressing regret for
any inadvertent error, will be happy to make the necessary correc-
tion in future printings. Thanks are due to the following for
permission to reprint the copyrighted material listed below:

Atheneum, Inc. for "The Witch's Garden". Text copyright © 1975
    by Lilian Moore. From SEE MY LOVELY POISON IVY.
    Used by permission of Atheneum Publishers.
Kenneth C. Bennett, Jr., for "The Witch of Willowby Wood" by
    Rowena Bennett.

Curtis-Brown, Ltd. for "This Witch" by Lee Bennett Hopkins. Copyright © 1977 by Lee Bennett Hopkins.

E. P. Dutton & Co., Inc. for "The Old Witch" and "Lazy Hans" by Ruth-Manning Sanders. From A BOOK OF WITCHES by Ruth Manning-Sanders. Copyright © 1966 by Ruth Manning-Sanders. Reprinted by permission of the publishers, E. P. Dutton. "The Witch in the Wintry Wood" by Aileen Fisher. From SPOOKS, SPIRITS AND SHADOWY SHAPES, edited by Elizabeth Yates. Copyright 1949 by E. P. Dutton, and reprinted with their permission. Used by permission of Methuen Publications, for Canadian rights.

Garrard Publishing Co. for "Beware" by Lee Blair from POETRY OF WITCHES, ELVES, AND GOBLINS selected by Leland B. Jacobs. Copyright © 1970 by Leland B. Jacobs.

Helen Finger Leflar for "The Magic Ball" by Charles J. Finger from TALES FROM SILVER LANDS by Charles J. Finger, Newbery Award winner, 1925.

Parents' Magazine Press for excerpt of "Ivashko and the Witch" from RUSSIAN TALES OF FABULOUS BEASTS AND MARVELS by Lee Wyndham. Text copyright © 1969 by Lee Wyndham. By permission of Parents' Magazine Press.

Penn Publishing Co. for "Peter and the Witch of the Wood" by Anna Wahlenberg from OLD SWEDISH FAIRY TALES.

Jean Conder Soule for "Grimelda." Used by permission of the author who controls all rights.

Viking Press for "Which Was Witch?" by Eleanore M. Jewett from WHICH WAS WITCH: TALES OF GHOSTS AND MAGIC FROM KOREA by Eleanore M. Jewett. Copyright 1953 by Eleanore Myers Jewett. Reprinted by permission of The Viking Press.

Library of Congress Cataloging in Publication Data
Main entry under title:

Witching time.

    SUMMARY: An anthology of stories and verses about
witches of the past and present.
    1. Witchcraft—Juvenile fiction. 2. Witchcraft—
Juvenile poetry. 3. Children's stories, American.
4. Children's stories, English. [1. Witches—Fiction.
2. Witches—Poetry] I. Hopkins, Lee Bennett.
II. Rosenberry, Vera.
PZ5.W7564   820'.8'0375   77-4742
ISBN 0-8075-9139-4

WITCHING TIME

Contents

Part Two:

A CAULDRON OF WICKED WITCHES

# Introduction

About Witching Time

What is a witch? Ask any twenty-five people what a witch is and you'll get twenty-five different answers, and a few scoffs and guffaws as well.

You've surely read about witches, and so you know they are evil creatures with special powers over those around them. There are wizards, too, with the same kind of power, but wizards are men and witches are women.

Witches (and the belief in them) have been around for a long time, centuries and centuries, even thousands of years. Witches have been around so long that storytellers and writers have woven many tales and poems about their wild and weird ways.

Almost everyone is fascinated by witches, but I have a special reason. My very own Great-grandmother Martha was said to have been a witch. Now this may have been because she was born on October 31, the perfect birthday for a Halloween witch.

The Halloween witch is the kind most of us think of when we hear the word "witch." Most Halloween witches look alike, dressed in black with long cloaks and pointed hats. They're old and ugly (usually), and their only companions are black cats. At night, alone or in a coven, Halloween witches astride their broomsticks ride through the skies.

Right here I want to say that Great-grandmother Martha was certainly old when I met her, but she was not ugly. She hated black dresses, and her cat was white. She didn't own a broom, and she swept her stoop with a vacuum cleaner. But sometimes her laugh was a cackle, and she just might have behaved like a witch on some occasions. Was she a witch? Perhaps not, but having a witch for a great-grandmother is something to consider. It reminds you that there are many kinds of witches, even young and beautiful ones. Some use spells to change themselves into all sorts of shapes, some are stupid, and some clever. Witches, in short, are as different as people.

Most witches, however, share one trait. They are mischievous. Sometimes they are mischievous and mean and horrid, or they can be mischievous in ways that seem funny to them but not to us.

In this collection of stories and poems, *Witching Time*, there are indeed many kinds of witches. They are found in tales that are very old and in others newly written.

The stories and poems are divided into two sections. In the first, called "A Brew of New Witches," you'll meet a variety of weird characters. There's a witch who wheezes for hours, one who lives in a house with lollipop shingles that are hurricane proof, and seven witches who sing Happy Birthday to themselves not once but seven times. One old crone is lonely and unhappy, and others have given up their broomsticks in favor of up-to-date ways.

The really mean, scheming witches are waiting in the second part of this book, "A Cauldron of Wicked Witches." Here are stories that have been told in England, Germany, Sweden, Russia, Korea, Ecuador, and the United States.

A cruel witch with iron teeth menaces a boy in a Russian folktale, while Hans, a cocky young man, talks back to a witch who would make him her servant. Two sisters have very different encounters with a blustering witch, while in the high Andes in South America, a brother and sister meet a cold-eyed, wrinkled creature, thin lipped, with hands like tree roots and skin so tough no arrow can pierce it.

Short tales and poems to read quickly, long stories to savor, they're all here to choose from. Some of the adventures will keep you in suspense until the last page and others will make you laugh or even cackle out loud like an old witch.

So now it's time to let yourself be bewitched. Just to be on the safe side, shun black cats and broomsticks for a while. Come along, it's time to read. It's *Witching Time.*

LEE BENNETT HOPKINS
Scarborough, New York

A brew of new
WITCHES

BEWARE

Beware the witch's magic glance!
      One look into her eye
Will turn you to a broomstick,
      To ride the midnight sky.

Beware the witch's magic brew,
      For but a taste of that
Will turn you quite immediately
      Into a big, black cat.

Beware the witch's magic power,
      Beware the witch's spell,
Lest when you'll be yourself again,
      Who can ever tell?
              Lee Blair

Frances Veirs

THE WITCHES' BIRTHDAY PARTY

Once, and not so long ago, there were seven witches who lived together in a big dark cave. With them lived their seven fiery-eyed black cats that arched their backs and yowled, because they didn't know how to purr.

The cave was a gloomy place for a home, but the witches liked it that way.

The seven witches looked exactly alike and they all had the same name, the same nickname, and the same birthday.

The way they looked was just horrible, but the witches liked it that way. They liked their sharp faces, hooked noses and snaggle teeth. They liked the tangled hair that got in their eyes.

The real name of these seven witches was *Scatterfright* and their nickname was *Scat*. They had to use numbers to keep from getting mixed up.

Their birthday was every Halloween and, like everybody else, they liked to have fun on their birthday. They thought the most fun in the world was scaring people.

One Halloween, when it was getting dark and children everywhere were putting on costumes to go to parties, six of the witches were sitting in the cave, making plans.

Scat Number Two said, "I'll tap on the windows and, when the people look up, I'll make a horrible face at them."

"You don't need to make a horrible face," said Scat Number Five. "You look horrible enough already."

"Thank you," said Scat Number Two. "That is quite the nicest compliment I ever had."

Scat Number Four said, "I'll sneak up behind people on the street and nudge them in the back. Think how scared they'll be when they see me!"

Scat Number Three said, "I'll make myself invisible and I'll laugh a horrible laugh. Like this . . . heh, heh, heh."

Then the witches were quiet. They were thinking up more ways to have fun. And they were wishing Scat Number One would hurry back. No doubt she would bring them some lovely ideas.

At last Scat Number One came sailing in on her broomstick. The other witches could hardly wait to find out what horrible new things she had in mind.

"Tell us about your trip," they said.

Scat Number One sat down and looked dreamy-eyed. The other witches thought she must be sick.

"I saw the usual things," she said. "Boys and girls going to Halloween parties, calling, 'Trick or treat.' But the most wonderful thing I saw was a little girl's birthday party."

"Birthday party?" echoed the other witches. "What's a birthday party? Is it something more horrible than we ever thought of?"

"It's a cake with candles and pink icing," said Scat Number One dreamily. "And ice cream. And pretty little things called favors. And they played games."

The other witches were amazed.

But now Scat Number One surprised them even more. She said, "I'm going to conjure up a birthday cake with candles and pink icing. And ice cream and favors. Tonight we'll stay home and have a birthday party!"

Then Scat Number One started conjuring. Instead of saying,

> *Shake and tremble, shake and tremble,*
> *Let the witches' brew assemble,*

she sang,

> *Happy birthday to me,*
> *Happy birthday to me,*
> *Happy birthday, dear Scatterfright,*
> *Happy birthday to me!*

Seven times she sang the happy birthday song. And then, on the big rock that usually held bitter brew, there appeared a lacy tablecloth, a beautiful birthday cake, seven dishes of strawberry ice cream, and seven little pink and white hats.

The other witches tasted the cake and nearly choked.

But when they tasted the ice cream, they decided this was even worse. Who could possibly eat anything *sweet?* The witches didn't want to be impolite, so they ate the candles.

Scat Number One tried hard to eat her cake. After all, she had conjured it up. But after five bites her face turned green.

"Maybe the cake and ice cream will taste better when they're old and moldy," she apologized. "Anyway, we can put on our hats and play games."

Scat Number One tried game after game. Everyone looked sadder and sadder, with the dainty pink and white hats perched on their scraggly heads.

Then suddenly Scat Number One took off her pink and white cap and shouted, *"Great snakes and smoking cauldrons! Who wants to have a silly old birthday party!"* She went straight to the hitching post and picked up her broomstick.

The other witches let out a cry of joy. They were going to have fun on their birthday, after all. Oh, what a night for flying!

They would tap on windows and make horrible faces at people. They would sneak up on people on the street. They would laugh —heh, heh, heh—in people's ears.

And right away seven proper witches went sailing through the air on their broomsticks—with seven cats sitting in front of them yowling, and bats flying around their heads. They *liked* it that way.

GRIMELDA

Jean Conder Soule

Of all the witches in Wicked Wood
The one who looked like a real witch should
Was Grimelda Snaggletooth Cobweb Claw,
The witchiest witch you ever saw.

Though all of her neighbors for many a mile
Lived in apartments of modern style
Grimelda preferred her old hollow tree,
Declaring her house the best place to be.

Now Grimelda's house was filled with things
Like spiders and mice and bats with wings.
They slept in her hat and her rocking chair
And dust and clutter was everywhere.

But Grimelda Snaggletooth Cobweb Claw
Didn't care a bit. She said, "Oh pshaw!
A witch's home is supposed to look
Like a haunted house in a storybook."

She hung out her wash on Hangman's Tree
Where all of the modern witches could see
Her patchy aprons and holey socks,
And often, her funny old-fashioned frocks.

"It's quite a disgrace to our neighborhood,"
Scoffed Wilma Witch. "I think we should
Get up a petition around the town.
Grimelda's tree should be taken down!"

"Agreed," said the other witches. "You're right.
Grimelda's house is a terrible sight.
She'll give us all a very bad name.
People will think we're all the same."

"I'll write a petition," said Cindera Smogg.
"Do you know she keeps a toad and a frog
And sixteen bats in her living room?
And she hasn't an automatic broom!"

"I'll be first to sign. You can count me in,"
Squeaked Sarah Screetch. "It's really a sin
The way she brews those wicked brews.
Have you ever smelled her bubbly stews?"

"If we make her stop, we'll have the solution
To half the county's air pollution,"
Said all of the witches short and tall.
Then they signed their names, both large and small.

Mag the Hag took charge of the crowd.
She screeched in a voice that was clear and loud,
"We'll give Grimelda one week from today;
By then she must pack and move away."

Later that day the witches began
To form their "OUT WITH GRIMELDA" plan.
They'd march to the tree on Witchcraft Row
And their signs would say: "GRIMELDA MUST GO!"

Now while the witches were planning their march
Grimelda was busily making starch
To stiffen the brim of her funny old hat.
She shooed out a mouse and a sleeping bat

Who were sound asleep in her old stew pot.
(For her starch was made in her old brew pot.)
After she'd finished that household chore
She took out a patchy old dress she wore

When she rode her broom last Halloween.
"That's quite the frumpiest one I've seen,"
Muttered Grimelda. "It's far from new;
But pooh! Who cares? It will have to do."

As she swished the starch with a vulture's feather
She happened to look outside at the weather.
"My!" she exclaimed. "The sky looks black."
Then she raised her rattly window a crack.

There from her house on Witchcraft Row
She saw puffs of smoke in the valley below.
Cried the startled witch, "I do declare!
The apartment house is on fire down there!"

"Girls! Your houses are all aflame!"
Grimelda shrieked as the witches came
Marching up to her house in line,
Each one holding a printed sign.

"Hurry! We've got to do something quick!
Now let me see—there's a magic trick
For putting out fires. I'm sure I knew it;
But I'm so excited I couldn't do it!"

"Help!" screamed Wilma. "My beautiful rooms!
My closets of clothes! My electric brooms!
They'll all burn up. Oh hurry, please do!
Call the Fire Department—Six—Seven—Five—Two!"

Grimelda hurriedly grabbed her switch
And off she flew like a jet-propelled witch.
The Fire Department had reached the spot
When Grimelda arrived, but the old witch got

The fancy clothes, the electric brooms
And the potions and pots from the burning rooms.
She made dozens of trips from the valley below
To her hollow tree on Witchcraft Row.

"Hooray for Grimelda!" the witches cried.
"We're glad to have her on our side.
She saved our treasures. She saved the day!
Grimelda, my dear, you are here to stay!"

Grimelda cackled and then she said,
As she took off the dented hat on her head,
"Now come inside and I'll brew some tea—
If you don't mind the clutter and dust, you see."

And not one witch either large or small
Uttered a single word at all
About patchy aprons or holey socks
Or Grimelda's funny old-fashioned frocks.

And Mag the Hag made a special sign
Printed in letters of fancy design—
UP WITH SPIDERS *and* UP WITH MICE!
THREE CHEERS FOR GRIMELDA—
         WE THINK SHE'S NICE!

THE WITCH'S GARDEN
Lilian Moore

In the witch's
garden
the gate is open
wide.

"Come inside,"
says the
witch.
"Dears,
come inside.

No flowers
in MY garden,
nothing mint-y
nothing chive-y

Come inside,
come inside.
See my lovely
poison ivy."

Gunhild Paehr

THE LONELY WITCH

Once upon a time there was an old witch, a very, very old witch, and she certainly looked her age. Her spells were still excellent, for witches never forget their magic however old they become. At night she still rode on her broomstick, though she did travel more and more slowly. The fast flights of her youth had become too much for her.

Her eyes, too, were no longer as sharp as they had once been and, when she spoke, her tone had become less sharp and sarcastic. But then she had never been a really wicked witch. She was not nearly as bad as some of them—cakes were all she baked in her kitchen oven.

Like most old witches, she lived in the forest in an ancient hovel which stood on the shore of a peaceful lake. The old witch led a quiet life there—in fact she found it almost too quiet.

With the passing of time all her old friends had moved out of the district. The neighboring witches had gone to the devil. The watersprite, who had once lived in the lake, had moved to different waters. So the old witch no longer had anyone to talk to and she felt very lonely.

The only other inhabitant of the forest was a robber. But he was no friend of hers—certainly not! She did not want to have anything to do with him. She had always earned her living honestly.

The witch did occasionally meet other people strolling through the forest. Many of them came from the town on Sundays in order to enjoy the fresh country air. They were ordinary friendly people who played their mouth organs and sang songs while the children picked flowers. The witch longed to make friends with them.

But all her efforts were unsuccessful. Nobody would have anything to do with her. Whenever they caught sight of her they would turn and run, just like the robber, while the children would shout, "Yah! You old witch!"

They were all afraid of her and that made the witch very unhappy.

"If only I knew how to make these people like me," she sighed. She brooded about it for a long time and at last decided to mix herbs into magic brews.

It was all in vain. People continued to be afraid and would have nothing to do with her. When they saw her they turned and ran, and when she waved to them they ran away faster than ever.

So the lonely old witch thought about her problem all over again, wondering what she could do to make people like her. She brooded about it for a long time and at last it occurred to her that children like sweets.

"I'll conjure up a magic gingerbread house," she decided. "That'll bring the children along, I'm sure."

No sooner said than done. She set about weaving the spell.

It was an enchanting little house. The walls were made of boiled sweets, cemented with marzipan. The roof was made of best nougat and the door was a solid slab of chocolate.

It was all in vain. Nobody came to eat the sweets.

On the contrary—the children ran away as soon as they caught sight of the little gingerbread house, and the grown-ups avoided it too. Even the robber lacked the courage to come closer. Despite his trade, he preferred not to lay hands on the witch's property.

So the little house stood there in the forest, empty and solitary, until the witch lost patience one day and spirited it away again.

She ceased to wonder what she could do to please people. In fact, she quite lost heart and gave up all hope of a new life.

"What's the use of wearing myself out," she thought in her despair. "They're all afraid of me."

Yet on the day when somebody finally did appear who was not afraid of her, she felt worse than ever.

A new gamekeeper moved into the gamekeeper's cottage. He was an unusually brave man and declared, "I mean to clear the forest of robbers and witches, so that people can stroll around here in peace."

That gave the old witch a shock! Now, in addition to all her other troubles, she had to start worrying about the future. What was to become of her if she were driven out of the forest at her age?

One night, as she was flying over the town, she saw two green lights glowing on the roof of the town hall.

"Must be a cat," she thought.

Full of curiosity, she guided her broomstick a little nearer.

The cat looked round and nodded to her amiably, so she took heart and asked, "May I sit with you for a while, cat? Or are you afraid of me?"

"Dear me, no," he purred. "Cats are never afraid of witches. Miaow. Not at all! I may be only a house cat, but my ancestors weren't so down to earth. Not by a long way. My late grandfather lived with a magician for many years."

The old witch propped her broomstick against a chimney pot and sat down with a sigh of relief.

"I do like a nice chat," she said, "but I don't often get the chance."

"Miaow, how sad. I don't like to be without friends," replied the cat.

"Yes, it's not much of a life," sighed the witch. "Human beings can't stand the sight of me. They all run away, and the children shout, 'Yah! You old witch!' Even the robber avoids me. It's enough to make one sick!"

The black cat studied her thoughtfully but kept quiet.

"The only one who's not afraid of me is the new gamekeeper," the old witch complained. "And that's worst of all. Imagine! He's threatened to clean up the woods. I can understand his wanting to give the robber notice, but what can he possibly have against me?"

The black cat raised his head as if he were about to speak, but he appeared to have second thoughts and went on keeping quiet.

"It's not as if I hadn't tried to be friendly," the old witch confided, and told the cat about the efforts she had made.

The black cat could keep quiet no longer.

"You conjured up a *gingerbread* house?" he burst out. "Miaow! Really, you're not very bright as witches go. Take my word for it, gingerbread houses have been out of date for a long time now. People buy their sweets in shops these days. Miaow! And anyway, children know what to expect from gingerbread houses. They've read all the fairy tales."

As the old witch didn't seem to get the point, he added, "Surely you've heard the story of Hansel and Gretel?"

"What sort of a witch do you take me for?" exclaimed the witch, outraged. "I certainly didn't mean any harm."

"But how were the children to know?" The black cat shook his head. "You'll never make friends that way. Miaow! You should set about it quite differently."

The old witch took heart. "What would you advise, cat?" she asked eagerly.

He hesitated. "May I speak quite frankly?"

"Please do," she said quickly.

"Now listen," he began carefully. "I would recommend that you pay more attention to your appearance. Because as you are now, it's really not surprising if . . . "

"If what?" asked the witch.

"Miaow, if people are afraid of you."

"Why?" asked the old witch.

The black cat wrung his paws in embarrassment. "Well, look in your mirror," he suggested shyly.

"I don't hold with such nonsense in *my* house," sniffed the old witch.

"Oh, I see." The black cat scratched an ear. This explained a lot.

The old witch grew impatient. "Now don't play cat and mouse with me, cat," she exclaimed.

So the cat decided to make himself clear. "Miaow. I don't want to offend you, but you really do look like an old witch."

"The nerve!" screeched the witch, thoroughly offended.

The black cat said no more. He was a peace-loving animal and considered quarreling beneath him.

"You can't get out of it now," cried the old witch, still very ruffled. "You'll have to see it through. What's wrong with me, anyway?"

What a question! The black cat looked her over from head to foot. M-i-a-o-w! Where should he start?

Her shoes were down at the heel. Her snagged stockings were wrinkled and full of holes. Her skirt was frayed, her blouse torn and stained. In a word, she was dressed in rags.

The black cat cleared his throat. "Tell me, witch, when did you last comb your hair?"

The old witch tried to remember. She reckoned it must have been about three or four months ago.

"Miaow! Miaow!" The black cat was shocked. "You'll have to comb your hair every morning from now on."

The old witch tittered. "You will have your little joke, cat."

"But I mean it," he assured her. "You should brush your hair regularly too, and get a good shine on it. After all, I clean my fur every day."

"We can't all be the same," muttered the witch.

"And why not try a new hair style?" continued the black cat. "Those long strands don't suit you at all. If I were you I'd go to a good hairdresser."

The old witch stared at him, flabbergasted.

"Miaow! And you ought to see a dentist, and . . . "

"My teeth don't hurt," she interrupted.

The black cat nodded. "That's what I mean. You haven't any."

"I have got one," the old witch contradicted him.

"That's not enough." And he continued, warming to his subject. "Last, but not least, I would advise you to have a really thorough wash."

A thorough wash? The witch shuddered. Fire and brimstone! What a horrible thought!

"Not just face and hands. Your neck, and behind your ears, too," urged the cat. "Best of all, why don't you climb straight into your tub and have a good hot soapy bath?"

"The idea!" shrieked the witch. "In all my born days I've never touched water."

"Miaow, that's only too obvious," commented the cat. "What's more, after your bath you must cut your fingernails. They're just like claws at present. And your clothes leave a lot to be desired."

The old witch gave a contemptuous sniff. "I suppose you want me to go around in silk or satin?"

"By no means," explained the cat. "That would be quite out of place and not your style at all."

The old witch wrinkled her nose. "Have you any more suggestions, cat?" she asked bitingly.

"Miaow, yes. Above all, make an effort to be a bit more agreeable. There's no need to look so cross all the time."

"We can't all grin like a lot of Cheshire cats," croaked the witch.

"Miaow, you shouldn't croak like that either," said the cat critically. "If you'll forgive my saying so, it sounds dreadful. After all, you've got the remedies at home. Why don't you take some of your own cough medicine?"

"Goodness," moaned the witch, "you *do* expect a lot from a poor old woman."

"You don't have to take my advice," said the black cat. "But I mean well and I'm only saying it for your own good. I know human beings and I know what they respect. Miaow, now, don't forget what the gamekeeper said. I'd think it all over if I were you."

The old witch did not say another word. She flew home on her broomstick and had a good think. She brooded for a long while. Finally she realized that she would have to do as the black cat had suggested if she really wanted to get on with people. It was the only way. Most important of all, she wanted to make a good impression on the gamekeeper. Then, maybe, he would take pity on her and let her stay in the forest.

Moaning and groaning, the old witch climbed into the tub and had a thorough wash. After her bath she cut her fingernails. A strong spell provided her with a new set of teeth. She tried to improve her voice by eating honey and drinking cough medicine. She even combed her hair, although she could not bring herself to have it curled. She felt that would have looked too youthful and decided on a neat bun instead. Next she darned her stockings and then bought herself new shoes. When, at last, she put on a pretty dress, she was completely transformed. In fact, the improvement was so great that she was unrecognizable.

Only the expression on her face still left a lot to be desired. But one could hardly expect an old witch to look friendly at her first attempt. After all, she had so far had very little practice at smiling.

Besides, her beauty treatment had left her worn out. She felt quite ill. She had indigestion from all the sweet things she had eaten. The hairpins stuck into her head, and the weight of the bun pulling her hair soon gave her a dreadful headache. In addition, she still had to get used to the new teeth.

Worst of all, the new shoes pinched her feet. The old witch soon had so many blisters that she could no longer take a walk in the forest. So she sat down outside her hut and hoped that people would come to her. But she hoped in vain. And the longer she waited the crosser she looked.

Occasionally people did come quite close, but no one wanted to visit her. They all turned and ran at the mere sight of her hut, while the children shouted, "Pooh! Look at that nasty old hovel!"

"Anyone would think I'd been bewitched," thought the old witch. "I'd better have another chat with the black cat."

As soon as it was dark she got out her broom. But this led to further exasperation when she discovered that she was hampered by her new skirt.

"Fire and brimstone!" she cursed. "Now I'll have to ride side-saddle!"

She flew along even more slowly than usual, sighing heavily as she went. Her good temper did not return until she had reached the town and seen the glitter from two green eyes on the roof of the town hall. The black cat was sitting there again.

The old witch landed beside him. "Good evening," she said.

The black cat looked up. "Miaow, may I ask with whom I have the honor of speaking?"

"Don't you recognize me?" asked the old witch, rather put out.

The black cat studied her from head to foot. Then he noticed the broomstick. "Well now, would you be a witch by any chance?"

She nodded. "Of course. *The* witch. I took your advice."

"M-i-a-o-w!" The black cat blinked. He could hardly believe his eyes. He would never have thought it possible.

"Am I so different?" asked the witch.

"Miaow, I should say so," he purred. "You look marvelous now. So clean!"

"I didn't do things by halves," answered the old witch. "I took a real bath. Ugh, fire and brimstone! Never again! It was torture."

"Your voice has changed completely, too," said the black cat approvingly. "It's so clear and not at all hoarse."

"I ate lots of honey and took cough medicine," explained the witch. "I'm feeling pretty sick now."

The black cat was still marveling. "And you're so charmingly dressed."

"Oh, I was so much more comfortable and easy in my rags," wailed the old witch. "And you can't imagine how these new shoes are pinching me."

"One has to suffer to be beautiful." The black cat knew all about it.

"Can you imagine it, in spite of all my efforts, human beings still won't have anything to do with me. They're still afraid of me."

"Miaow, that's odd," commented the cat.

"Yes, it's too awful," complained the witch. "They all run away at the mere sight of my hut, while the children shout, 'Pooh, look at that nasty hovel!'"

The black cat pricked up his ears.

"I just can't understand it. It's really very pleasant at home and there's such a lovely view from my windows. Did I tell you that I live by the lake?"

"Miaow," the black cat cleared his throat. "Tell me, what's your house like?"

"It's fiendishly comfortable," said the witch. "The walls are full of dry rot and the roof has almost caved in. The floors all creak and the wind howls down the chimney. And I've plenty of company. There are bats nesting in the attic and there are rats gnawing away in the cellar."

"I see." The black cat scratched an ear. This explained a lot.

"And you should just see my furniture!" cried the old witch with glee. "Most of the chair backs are missing and the cupboards are worm-eaten. But the kitchen is the coziest place of all. It's got that lovely fire-and-brimstone smell."

"Miaow! Miaow!" thought the black cat, horrified. He asked hesitantly, "May I speak quite frankly?"

"Please do," she said quickly.

"If I were you I'd get myself a new house," he murmured.

The old witch laughed. "You're joking, cat," she said.

"Miaow, I'm perfectly serious," he assured her.

"That's just the sort of idea you would have," scolded the witch. "What's the point of having a new hut?"

The black cat decided to make himself clear. "Miaow, I don't want to offend you, but you really can't entertain in such an old ruin."

"The nerve!" screeched the witch, outraged.

"Now you're screeching again," the black cat said reproachfully.

"You can't get out of it now," cried the old witch, very ruffled. "You'll have to tell me the rest. What's wrong with my hut anyway?"

What a question!

"If you don't mind my saying so, everything," answered the black cat. "It really ought to be pulled down."

The old witch stared at him, flabbergasted.

"Miaow, a new house wouldn't cost you a thing. After all, you can use magic. Don't you think a modern house would be enchanting? With red gables and a large sun parlor, running water and central heating?"

The old witch sniffed in contempt. She didn't hold with such newfangled nonsense.

"I would also recommend a kitchen with built-in cupboards," continued the black cat. "You can't imagine how convenient they are. And for each room you should conjure up some new furniture. I'd burn the old stuff if I were you. It's not worth selling."

The old witch would have liked to contradict him but he didn't give her time to interrupt. "You could hang some attractive pictures on the walls and some curtains at the windows."

"Any other suggestions?" asked the old witch icily.

"Miaow," the black cat nodded his head eagerly. "You could lay out some flower beds and a lawn in front of the house. And you could set garden furniture on the lawn—some of those pretty chairs, a table and a gay umbrella."

"Goodness," moaned the witch. "You do expect a lot from a poor old woman."

"You don't have to take my advice," said the cat. "But I mean well and I'm only saying it for your own good. I know human beings, believe me, and I know what they respect. Miaow! And don't forget what the gamekeeper said. I'd think it all over if I were you."

The old witch raised no further objections. She flew home on her broomstick and had a good think.

The old witch brooded for a long while and finally realized that

she would have to do as the black cat suggested if she really wanted
to get on with people. It was the only way. Most important of all, she
wanted to make a good impression on the gamekeeper. He had
already begun to search the forest. Woe betide her if she aroused his
dislike. He would send her away at once.

So the witch used her magic to provide herself with a modern
house with red gables and a large sun parlor. She installed running
water but could not bring herself to put in central heating. She
felt that would really be too modern and decided on a tiled stove
instead.

Next she furnished all her rooms with brand-new furniture. She
hung pictures on the walls and curtains at all the windows.

"I only hope it'll be worth all the bother," she sighed.

When she had finished furnishing the house the old witch began to
lay out her garden. She saw to it that flower beds and a lawn
appeared in next to no time. On the lawn she set a table, some pretty
chairs and a gay garden umbrella.

Finally, she quickly ran a comb through her hair, for the hard
work had untidied her new hairstyle. Then she hopefully sat down
in the shade of the umbrella to wait for company.

This time she did not wait in vain. Visitors arrived that very
afternoon.

It so happened that a man and his wife had gone for a walk by the
lake. When they saw the pretty new house they did not turn back.
On the contrary, they came closer to have a good look at it. Then,
when they noticed the large sun parlor, the gay umbrella and the

attractive furniture they said, "How charming! It must be an open-air restaurant."

It was an understandable mistake. After all, private houses do not usually stand in the depths of a forest.

So they decided to go in.

The old witch jumped up and hurried to meet them.

"So pleased to meet you," she cried, almost croaking with excitement. "How kind of you to call on me. May I offer you a little refreshment? A glass of herbal tea, perhaps?"

The couple exchanged a glance. "We'd rather have coffee and cakes," they said, "but may we see the menu first, please?"

Menu? The old witch gazed at them, baffled.

"We'd like to know how much the coffee costs," explained the man.

The old witch laughed. "Why, you'll be my guests, of course," she assured them.

"Your guests? But aren't you the owner?"

"Owner?" The old witch looked blank.

"But you must have a menu," cried the woman.

"What for?" asked the witch.

Once more the couple exchanged a glance. "You've probably only just opened the place," they said. "Perhaps you don't have much restaurant experience."

At last the old witch understood what had happened. She did not dare to contradict them, however, let alone have them find out who she was. So she went off to her kitchen.

She brewed some strong coffee in her cauldron and, as there was no time for her to bake cakes, she used a spell and transformed a gust of wind into cream puffs.

The visitors were delighted with the restaurant. They praised the service. "That coffee was excellent—really strong. And the cream puffs were delicious. We've never tasted anything like them before."

The old witch nodded. She could well believe it.

"We'll be back again next Sunday," they decided.

The old witch nodded. That was what she had been hoping to hear.

"An open-air restaurant is just what was needed in the forest," said the woman.

"We like to stop for refreshments when we're taking a long walk," explained the man.

The old witch nodded again. How well they were getting on together! They were just like old friends.

Suddenly the old witch did not find it at all difficult to look friendly. Everything went smoothly until the visitors asked the witch the best way back to the town.

"Keep going straight on," replied the old witch. "You can't possibly miss the way."

"Is it quite safe?" asked the woman.

"Safe?" repeated the old witch. "Why shouldn't it be safe?"

The woman lowered her voice. "We're afraid of meeting that wicked old witch," she murmured.

"What's that?" screeched the witch.

"Good gracious! Don't you know about her?" The couple were amazed.

"No," cried the old witch. "I certainly don't know a wicked old witch."

"Of course, I was forgetting you only moved here recently," said the man. "Naturally you wouldn't know anything about it. But listen, there's an old witch living somewhere near here."

"Old witch!" muttered the witch. "Old witch! The idea!"

"Do be careful if you come across her," the woman warned her. "She's terrifying—and ugly enough to frighten anyone out of their wits. She must be the worst witch in the world."

The old witch was speechless. She was too angry to utter a word. To think that she had to listen to such insults, and in her own house too. The witch went on raging long after the people had gone and, as soon as it was dark, she took her broom and flew to the town. She wanted to have another word with the black cat.

The witch's luck was in. She could see his green eyes gleaming a long way off.

The old witch galloped up. She was so distressed she even forgot to say good evening.

"Just think, cat," she gasped, "I've had visitors."

"Miaow, glad to hear it," he purred.

"But just wait till I tell you what happened," wailed the witch. And she told him how the people had mistaken her house for an open-air restaurant.

"You don't say!" grinned the cat.

"You can laugh." The old witch laid aside her broomstick and settled down next to him crossly.

The black cat shook his head. "You're a funny sort of witch. One minute you complain because people don't come near you and the next you complain because they do. What is it that you really want?"

"I want to be treated decently. If you'd only heard what they said to me. They called me a terrifying old witch."

"Miaow?" The cat twitched his whiskers. "They said that to your face?"

The old witch admitted that the people hadn't recognized her.

"Then you mustn't take it to heart so much," comforted the black cat. "It's no good being too sensitive. I should know, being a cat. I don't know how often I and my relatives have been called names. If it's not spiteful cat, it's something worse. Miaow, if I took it to heart each time I'd never get over it," he said.

"I'm not as thick-skinned as you are," muttered the witch.

The black cat decided to overlook this remark. "Do you know what I think?" he miaowed. "If I were you I'd really open an open-air restaurant."

The old witch gazed at him in astonishment.

"You will have your little joke, cat."

"Miaow, I mean it," he assured her. "I think it's a splendid idea. Think of it—then you'll always have company."

"That's just the sort of idea you would have," scolded the old witch. "Am I to rush around serving people at my age? Goodness knows I'm not as young as I used to be."

"It wouldn't be any real trouble," the cat assured her. "After all, you can call on magic. Besides, your house is ideal for the purpose."

"What a purpose!" grumbled the witch.

"You don't have to take my advice," said the black cat. "But I mean well and I'm only saying it for your own good. I know human beings, believe me, and I know what they respect. Miaow! I'd think it over if I were you."

The old witch raised no further objections. She flew home on her broomstick and had a good think. She brooded a long while, wondering whether to take the black cat's advice or not, and meanwhile, more visitors arrived.

In fact, the next batch of visitors appeared on the following day. Word had gone round the town that an open-air restaurant had been opened in the forest by the lake. In order to keep her visitors happy, the old witch hastily set up more tables, chairs and umbrellas on the lawn.

All the customers asked for cream puffs, for rumor had it that the cream puffs were particularly good and fresh in this open-air restaurant.

In fact, they were all quite delighted with everything and promised to tell all their friends about the place. "We'll be back next Sunday," they told the witch.

Even so, the old witch might still have changed her mind about running a restaurant if the gamekeeper had not paid her a visit.

True, he came on business. He had been searching the woods for the robber and the witch without success, so he naturally decided to give the new open-air restaurant a quick examination. He wanted to make sure that the robber was not hiding there.

The old witch had a dreadful shock when the gamekeeper suddenly arrived. "Oh dear," she thought. "Now he'll turn me out."

But this idea never even entered his head. How was he to recognize the old witch? Actually she made a very good impression on him.

"It's so cozy here," he thought. He admired the garden, the sun parlor and the lovely view of the lake. In fact he was delighted with everything. "This is the sort of place I like," he said. He patted the witch on the back in a friendly way and promised to come back soon. "Just carry on as you've begun," he said.

The gamekeeper's wish was her law. Now the old witch had no choice. She was forced to go on serving refreshments.

In order to avoid as much hard work as possible the witch did not even begin to cook or bake. She relied on magic in her kitchen. Soon she had grown quite used to her new life. As long as nobody mentioned wicked witches she liked having lots of visitors, although she still found it difficult to look friendly all the time.

On Sundays people came crowding in. The old witch was rushed off her feet. She could have done with ten hands and feet.

From all sides people clamored for service. Women cried, "It's my turn!" Men shouted, "Where's my coffee?"

The witch wasn't used to such an uproar. It made her feel quite nervous. She got so flustered that she began to go too fast. She started casting spells before she was alone in her kitchen.

At once there was a whistling, rushing sound. Customers were astonished to see cups and plates flying through the air and then landing on their tables. Ice cream, milk jugs and teapots sailed after them—not to mention coffeepots.

This caused quite a sensation. Many people took flight. Some of them ran to the gamekeeper and lodged a complaint.

"Gamekeeper! Gamekeeper! We wish to complain!" they all shouted at once.

"Now then, what's going on here?" he asked, stroking his beard.

"It's the new restaurant!" They shuddered. It was all too dreadful.

"It's terrifying!" A fat lady buried her face in her hands. "When I think of those saucers flying through the air!"

The gamekeeper smiled a superior smile. "There are no such things as flying saucers," he informed her. "That is an optical illusion. You have been misled by appearances."

"Is that so?" The fat lady snorted. "I was nearly knocked out by one."

"We can assure you that there's something wrong about that new restaurant, gamekeeper," cried all the others. "We don't have to wait for service. Everything comes flying at once. Suddenly there's a whistling, rushing sound and a glass of lemonade lands on the table. Then there are more rushing noises and cups and plates arrive. What's more, ice cream, milk jugs, and teapots sail through the air—not to mention coffeepots!"

The gamekeeper shook his head. "You've been out in the sun too long, that's what's the matter with you."

"What do you take us for?" they cried. "Take our word for it, that owner casts magic spells. We're sure she's the old witch."

The gamekeeper was still doubtful. The owner had made the best possible impression on him. "I'm sure the old witch has moved away," he muttered.

"How do you know for certain?" asked the fat lady.

The others cried, "Witches can change their shapes. We want you to investigate this open-air restaurant. We're not going to a place run by a wicked old witch, even if the cakes are particularly good and cheap."

"We might never get home again," wailed the fat lady. "What's to stop the witch from putting a spell on us?"

After a while the gamekeeper began to have serious doubts. Could he have made a mistake? He promised to go and see the owner.

As a matter of fact, the gamekeeper was doubly mistaken, about the robber as well as the old witch. They were both still in the forest. The robber had only gone into hiding in his lair for a while in order to keep out of the way of the law.

It was only after the gamekeeper had given up the search that the robber dared come out into the open again. Then he discovered the restaurant. And, as is the way of robbers, he began to plan sinister deeds.

Of course, if he had had the slightest idea who the owner was, he would have given up his plan at once. But the robber said to himself, "A full restaurant means a full cashbox. And a full cashbox means that there's a job for me to do."

So, on that very Sunday evening, he crept up to the witch's house and lurked about outside.

Meanwhile all the visitors had long since gone. Needless to say, the robber had no idea why they had left so early. So he thought, "Oho! The coast is clear! That old owner appears to be alone. I'll deal with her easily. Here we go!"

At first the old witch thought he was just another visitor. Her eyes weren't as sharp as they had been when she was younger.

She asked politely, "What can I get you?"

"Your money or your life," cried the robber.

"Oh—it's you!" cried the witch indignantly. "What do you mean by coming here, you crook? This is a respectable establishment. Robbers are forbidden here. Get out at once, you rascal, you thief, you swindler."

"I want to know where you keep your cash," yelled the robber.

"My cashbox is in that cupboard," she said craftily.

The robber didn't need to be told twice. He rushed to the cupboard, broke it open and began to search the shelves. In his greed he crept right inside.

This was just what the old witch had been waiting for.

"I'll teach you, you rascal," she thought. Then she murmured a spell:

> "Abracadabra, one, two, three,
> Where you are you stay—
> Until the time when I decree
> That you shall go away."

There was a crash. The door slammed and the robber was a prisoner.

"Let me out!" he shouted. "Help! Help! Let me out!"

But what was the use of shouting? The old witch merely covered her ears with her hands and did not listen.

"Fire and brimstone!" gasped the witch. "I must go and tell the black cat what has happened."

She fetched her broom from the cupboard and got ready to ride to the town.

But before she could leave the house the gamekeeper arrived.

"Gamekeeper, what an honor!" The old witch laid aside her broom and hurried to meet him. "How kind of you to visit me. What can I offer you? Perhaps a glass of lemonade?"

"No thanks," the gamekeeper said, and today he did not pat her on the back but said shortly, "I'm afraid there have been complaints about you."

"Complaints?" asked the old witch, crestfallen. "Have I kept my customers waiting?"

"No, on the contrary. You're too quick. People are saying that you make magic and that this proves your identity. They are sure you are the witch."

The old witch turned pale. She did not know what "identity" meant, but she felt sure it must be something bad.

The gamekeeper began to question her. "Do saucers really fly through the air here?"

"It could happen anywhere," stammered the old witch.

"Not in a respectable house," declared the gamekeeper sternly. "I am told that ice creams, milk jugs and teapots sail through the air—to say nothing of coffeepots."

"It does happen at times when I'm rushed," admitted the old witch.

The gamekeeper frowned. "That proves you use magic, and therefore you are a wicked witch."

"You're wrong," the witch objected. "I'm not wicked."

"Don't try to deny it," said the gamekeeper. "You can't pull the wool over *my* eyes. Now listen! I hereby order you to leave the wood. Your house will be taken away from you."

What a dreadful shock for the old witch! "Have mercy on me, gamekeeper," sobbed the witch. "It would be the end of me. It's hard to pull up one's roots at my age."

But the gamekeeper refused to change his mind and turned to go.

Suddenly he paused. He had heard something which sounded like someone muttering. He grew suspicious. He, too, had heard the story of Hansel and Gretel. A witch was capable of any wickedness, he knew, so he stopped and listened.

A voice could be heard quite clearly. It seemed to come from inside the cupboard.

"Help! Help! Let me out of here! I'm suffocating. Help! Help!"

The gamekeeper stiffened. "Who is shut up in that cupboard?" he asked the old witch.

"Only the robber," said the witch casually, continuing to wipe the tears from her eyes.

"What?"

"Self-defense," explained the old witch. "Imagine! That scoundrel tried to break into my house—the rascal, the thief, the swindler."

"You've locked up the robber?" The gamekeeper stroked his beard. Good heavens! He'd nearly made a dreadful mistake. How he had wronged the owner! It would have been unforgivable if he had sent away such a credit to the district.

The robber began to shout again. "Help! Help! I'm suffocating! Let me out!"

The gamekeeper remembered his duty. "Look here," he said, "the robber can't stay in your cupboard forever. He must go to prison."

"Would you like me to send him there for you with a spell?"

"Could you really?" cried the gamekeeper. "That would save a lot of trouble. It wouldn't even be necessary to arrest him."

"It's quite easy, really," said the old witch. "Just a moment . . . " and she murmured a magic spell:

"Abracadabra, one, two, three,

Robber—on your way!

Fly to prison—it's going to be

A rather lengthy stay."

At once there was a click. The door of the cupboard opened and out whirled the robber on his way to the nearest prison.

And he's probably still sitting there.

The gamekeeper thanked the old witch warmly. Then he looked embarrassed and told her how very sorry he was to have misjudged her.

The old witch blushed with joy. "Then you won't turn me out?" she stammered.

The gamekeeper shook her hand. "My dear, you don't think I would turn a good fairy out of the forest, do you?"

Good fairy? The old witch was taken aback.

"Aha!" said the gamekeeper. "I see you wish to hide your true identity."

The old witch blushed. She still did not know what "identity" meant, but now she felt sure it must be something good.

"You don't want people to know who you are," the gamekeeper told her with a smile. "But you can't pull the wool over *my* eyes. I wasn't born yesterday. A wicked witch would never have locked up a robber. Therefore you can't be a wicked witch."

The old witch nodded. Wasn't that just what she had been saying?

The gamekeeper winked at her confidentially. "But if you make magic spells and you aren't a wicked witch, then you must be a good fairy."

"You're wrong," the old witch contradicted him.

The gamekeeper chuckled. "Don't try to deny it. It's no use trying to fool me. And, now I come to think of it, that's why the wicked witch has disappeared. You must have driven her away. There's no doubt about it. You must be an extra specially good fairy."

The old witch did not dare to contradict him any longer. She minded very much being taken for a good fairy, but what could she do?

Besides, it was quite an advantage. Now she could make magic as much as she liked. No one would ever worry again if there was a whistling rushing sound and plates and cups landed on the table. Let alone if ice cream, milk jugs and teapots came sailing through the air—not to mention coffeepots.

The customers would even keep calm if it rained whipped cream. They would merely say, "After all, good fairies have their little ways."

From that day on, the open-air restaurant was crowded even on weekdays, and the gamekeeper himself became a regular customer.

But the old witch still found it hard to look friendly all the time. Her greatest pleasure was her nightly ride on the broomstick when she could relax after her busy day and not bother to keep up appearances.

The old witch and the black cat used to meet regularly on the roof of the town hall and, because she was grateful to him for his good advice, she called her open-air restaurant "The Black Cat."

THE WITCH OF WILLOWBY WOOD

Rowena Bennett

There once was a witch of Willowby Wood,
and a weird wild witch was she, with hair that was snarled
and hands that were gnarled, and a kickety, rickety
knee. She could jump, they say,
to the moon and back, but this I never did see.

Now Willowby Wood was near Sassafras Swamp,
where there's never a road or rut. And there by the
singing witch-hazel bush the old woman builded
her hut. She builded with neither a hammer or shovel.
She kneaded, she rolled out, she baked
her brown hovel. For *all* witches' houses, I've oft heard
it said, are made of stick candy and fresh
gingerbread. But the shingles that shingled this old
witch's roof were lollipop shingles and hurricane-proof,
too hard to be pelted and melted by rain.
(Why this is important I soon will explain.)

One day there came running to Sassafras Swamp a dark
little shadowy mouse. He was noted for being a scoundrel
and scamp. And he gnawed at the old woman's house
where the doorpost was weak and the doorpost was worn.
And when the witch scolded, he laughed her to scorn.
And when the witch chased him, he felt quite delighted.
She never could catch him for she was nearsighted. And
so, though she quibbled, he gnawed and he nibbled.

The witch said, "I won't have my house
take a tumble. I'll search in my magical book for a spell
I can weave and a charm I can mumble to get you
away from this nook. It will be a good warning to other
bad mice, who won't earn their bread
but go stealing a slice."
"Your charms cannot hurt," said the mouse, looking pert.

Well, she looked in her book and she
waved her right arm, and she said the most magical
things. Till the mouse, feeling strange,
looked about in alarm, and found he was growing some
wings. He flapped and he fluttered the longer she
muttered.

"And now, my fine fellow,
you'd best be aloft," said the witch as he floundered
around. "You can't stay on earth and you
can't gnaw my roof. It's lollipop-hard and it's
hurricane-proof. So you'd better take off
from the ground. If you are wise, stay in the skies."

Then in went the woman of Willowby Wood,
in to her hearthstone and cat.
There she put her old volume up high on the shelf, and
fanned her hot face with her hat. Then she said,
"That is *that!* I have just made a *bat!*"

A cauldron of
wicked WITCHES

THIS WITCH
Lee Bennett Hopkins

This sneezy, wheezy,
    scratchy, itchy,
    sneezy, wheezy,
    itchy
        witch

    sneezed from flowers,
    wheezed for hours,

    scratched so lively,
    itched from ivy,

    sneezed and wheezed,
    scratched and itched,
    sneezed and wheezed
        and
    itched, itched, itched.

This sneezy, wheezy
    scratchy, itchy,
    sneezy, wheezy,
    itchy
        witch.

Lee Wyndham

IVASHKO AND THE WITCH

In a certain village, not near, not far, not high, not low, there lived an old couple with one little son named Ivashko. They loved him so dearly, he was scarcely allowed out of their sight for fear harm might come to him.

One day Ivashko said to his parents, "I'd like to go fishing. There must be lots of fish in the lake in the woods. I could catch some for you."

"What are you thinking of! You're much too young to go to the woods by yourself," his father exclaimed. "There are all sorts of wild beasts and witches—"

"Besides, you might fall into the lake and drown!" His mother turned pale at the thought of such dangers.

But Ivashko begged and pleaded, teased and cried. So at last his father hollowed out a little boat for him from a thick log, and made him a fishing rod from a willow wand. His mother dressed him in a snow-white shirt and tied a red sash around his waist.

Both parents took him through the woods to the lake. They kissed him and blessed him. Ivashko climbed into his little dugout boat, and they pushed it into the water and went home.

It was then Ivashko discovered that his father had forgotten to make him oars. "I'll manage, anyway," he said, and sang out:

> *Little boat, little boat, float out a bit farther.*
> *Little boat, little boat, float out a bit faster!*

And it did. Ivashko began to fish and put his catch into the boat.

A short time later, his old mother hobbled down to the water's edge and called her son in a sweet, fond voice:

> *Ivashko, Ivashko, my dear son,*
> *Float back to shore;*
> *I've brought you food*
> *And I've brought you drink.*

Ivashko heard her and said:

> *Little boat, little boat, float back to shore.*
> *That's my mother calling and I must go to her.*

The boat floated to the shore. His mother gave him his food and drink and took the string of fish he had caught. Then she pushed the little boat out into the lake and went home.

Again Ivashko sang out:

> *Little boat, little boat, float out a bit farther.*
> *Little boat, little boat, float out a bit faster!*

The dugout floated off, and Ivashko dropped his line and began to fish. A short time later, his old father hobbled down to the water's edge and called his son in a thin, sing-song voice:

> *Ivashko, Ivashko, my dear son,*
> *Float back to shore;*
> *I've brought you food*
> *And I've brought you drink.*

And Ivashko said:

> *Little boat, little boat, float back to shore.*
> *That's my father calling and I must go to him.*

The boat floated to the shore. His father took the string of fish the boy had caught, gave him his food and drink, and then pushed the little boat out into the lake and went home.

• • •

Now a certain witch, named Lueda-yedka, heard Ivashko's parents calling him. Curious, she hurried to the lake and peered through the bushes. And there was Ivashko, rocking gently in his little dugout in the middle of the lake. Such a tender pink and white boy he was. Lueda-yedka's ugly mouth watered—for she was a witch who ate people. Even her name meant "people-eater." How she longed to get hold of this morsel! She crept closer to the bank and cried out in her hoarse, ugly voice:

> IVASHKO, IVASHKO, MY DEAR BOY,
> FLOAT BACK TO SHORE.
> I'VE BROUGHT YOU FOOD
> AND I'VE BROUGHT YOU DRINK.

Ivashko was so startled, he nearly fell out of his boat. *That* wasn't his father. And it certainly could not be his mother. The dreadful bray could only be the voice of a witch! He pretended that he had heard nothing and he sang out softly:

> *Little boat, little boat, float out a bit farther.*
> *Little boat, little boat, float out a bit faster.*
> *That is not my father, nor my dear mother,*
> *But a witch who calls me*
> *And I won't go to her.*

"*N'yah!*" snarled the witch. "The little brat is not easily fooled. I'll call him with a voice just like his mother's, and then he'll come to shore." She gnashed her iron teeth, tightened the rope belt around her hungry middle, and hurried to the blacksmith in the village.

"*Kuznetz!* Smith!" she rasped. "Make me a voice box that will sound as sweet and fond as the voice of Ivashko's mother. If you don't, I will eat you."

Trembling with terror, the smith forged her a voice box, and when they tried it, it sounded exactly like the voice of Ivashko's mother.

Lueda-yedka rushed back to the lake, held her voice box up, and it sang out:

> *Ivashko, Ivashko, my dear boy,*
> *Float back to shore;*
> *I've brought you food*
> *and I've brought you drink.*

Now that surely is my dear mother's voice, thought Ivashko. He spoke to his little boat, and obediently it floated to shore.

Lueda-yedka sprang out from the bushes, seized the boy with one hand and the fish he had caught with the other, and loped off into the woods. No matter how Ivashko pummeled and kicked, he could not loosen her clawlike hold on him.

When she reached her crooked hut, Lueda-yedka kicked the door open, flung the fish to her scrawny cat and thrust the boy into a stout iron cage. Then she bellowed for her only daughter:

"A-LEN-KA!"

Alenka came running—the spittle image of her ugly mother. "Yes, mama? Aaahhh! *Dinner!*" she screeched, and pranced round the iron cage, poking and pinching Ivashko.

"Stop your funning. Make a fire in the stove, stupid girl," the witch shouted. "Make the oven hot as can be and roast me that brat, while I go to invite some friends for the feast."

Alenka's evil eyes glittered as she followed her mother's orders. The stove got hotter and hotter. When she opened the iron door, a great wave of heat rolled out.

"Now then, little fellow," Alenka roared happily as she yanked Ivashko out of the cage. "Come here and sit on this shovel so I can put you in properly."

Though frightened nearly out of his mind, young Ivashko used what wits were left to him. "Shovel?" He looked puzzled. "I have never yet sat on a shovel. Won't you show me how to do it?"

"It's simple," Alenka assured him. "It won't take you any time to learn. Here, you hold it and I'll show you."

But the moment she sat on the shovel, Ivashko gave it a heave,

pitched her into the oven and slammed the iron door shut. He ran out of the hut, locked the door and threw away the key. Then, lickety-split, he climbed up into the top of a huge oak tree nearby.

And not a moment too soon, for the witch was returning. He could hear her rough voice and hoarse laughter as she and her guests crashed through the woods.

When the ugly crowd reached the hut, Lueda-yedka pushed at the door and found it locked. She pounded and kicked it and shouted to her daughter, but of course there was no reply.

"Oh, that lazy good-for-nothing!" Lueda-yedka shrieked. "She must have gone off to amuse herself—"

At that moment an acorn fell from Ivashko's tree and hit the witch on the head.

"ALENKA!" the witch bellowed. "This is no time for games! I smell the roast burning. Get down at once!" She looked up, but instead of her daughter, saw Ivashko clinging to the topmost branches.

With a horrible cry, Lueda-yedka spun about and lunged at the door. There was a crash, and the door flew apart in a shower of splinters. The witch rushed inside to peer into the oven.

"AAAAAAAAAAIE!" Shrieking, she rushed out again in a frenzy. She threw herself at Ivashko's oak and began to gnaw at the trunk. She had gnawed halfway through it when two of her iron teeth broke off with a twang.

"Don't let him get away!" she yelled to her guests and sped off to the village.

Once there, she rushed to the blacksmith. "*Kuznetz!* Smith! Make me some iron teeth. If you don't, I'll eat you!"

So the smith forged two iron teeth and hammered them into her jaw, and she rushed back to gnawing the oak tree again.

Ivashko was trapped. He looked up to heaven, and there was a flock of swan-geese approaching. Ivashko stretched out his arms beseechingly.

> *Oh, dear swans, oh, dear geese,*
> *Take me up on your wings,*
> *Carry me to my father's house*
> *Where my mother awaits me.*

But the swan-geese gave no sign of having heard him. The dreadful gnawing below was like a rasping saw, and the oak tree was beginning to groan and sway. Soon it would crash to the ground. Ivashko closed his eyes and prayed. When he opened them, the flock of swan-geese had almost flown past.

And then, all at once, a great white swan swooped out of the sky and flew straight down to Ivashko. The boy grasped the bird by the neck and swung up on its back. Away they flew—just as the mighty oak fell, SMASH! on top of the witch. It squashed her quite flat—and her ugly friends with her.

The great swan carried Ivashko all through the night. As the sun rose, the boy looked down—and there was the lake, and his little boat bobbing on it. Someone had tied it up to a birch tree. And there was his father's house. The swan glided down to the thatched roof.

Ivashko slid off the broad back. Before he could thank the great bird, it soared up into the sky and was gone to catch up with the flock.

Ivashko smelled breakfast cooking and heard the sound of weeping inside the cottage.

"What *could* have happened to our dear son?" his mother was sobbing. "Where *is* my Ivashko?"

"There, there," Ivashko heard his father say. "Perhaps the lad only wandered off. You know how boys are."

"Well, sit down and eat," said the mother. "I have made a stack of pancakes, though I could scarcely see to turn them through my tears. Here's one for you, and here's one for me. One for you, one for me."

Ivashko rolled to the edge of the roof, jumped to the ground and ran into the little house. "And what about me?" he shouted. "Don't I get any?"

His parents jumped up and hugged him and kissed him and laughed and cried. Then his mother fed him and hugged him and kissed him and laughed and cried. And after that, Ivashko was able to tell them everything that had happened.

"And now that the witch is dead," he said, "and won't be up to her tricks, I'd like to go back to my fishing."

And he did.

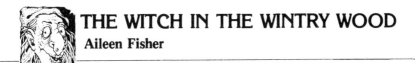

THE WITCH IN THE WINTRY WOOD
Aileen Fisher

This is the story of timid Tim
who thought that witches went after him
when the night was dark and the moon was dim.
   Woo-HOO, woo-HOO, woo-HOO.

This is the tale of how Tim one night
didn't start home until candlelight
when the sky was black and the snow was white.
   Woo-HOO, woo-HOO, woo-HOO.

He walked through the woods like a frightened goat,
his muffler twisted around his throat,
expecting to jump at a witch's note:
   "Woo-HOO, woo-HOO, woo-HOO."

Out of the night came a sheep dog's yowl,
which Tim was sure was a witch's howl,
a terrible witch on a wintry prowl.
   Woo-HOO, woo-HOO, woo-HOO.

Tim, the timid, began to race,
certain he sighted a witch's face
back of each shadowy hiding place.
   Woo-HOO, woo-HOO, woo-HOO.

He ran through the woods on his lonely trek
till horrors! a hand went around his neck,
holding his headlong flight in check.
   Woo-HOO, woo-HOO, woo-HOO.

Around his throat went a witch's hand
that jerked poor Tim to a sudden stand.
His heart was water, his legs were sand!
   Woo-HOO, woo-HOO, woo-HOO.

Nobody knows how long he stood
with that hand on his throat in the silent wood
until he could find some hardihood . . .
   Woo-HOO, woo-HOO, woo-HOO.

Then he looked around like a shaky calf,
thinking of words for his epitaph,
and "Oh, ho, ho!" he began to laugh . . .
   Woo-HOO, woo-HOO, woo-HOO.

For what he saw was a funny sight—
it *wasn't* a witch at his throat by night,
but a pine branch pulling his muffler tight!
   Woo-HOO, woo-HOO, woo-HOO.

The more Tim chuckled, the more he thought
how most of his fears were like mufflers caught
and stretched much tighter than mufflers ought.
Woo-HOO, woo-HOO, woo-HOO.

And the end of this story of timid Tim
is—nevermore, when the night was dim,
did he fear that witches were after him!
Woo-HOO, woo-HOO, woo-HOO.

Ruth Manning-Sanders
THE OLD WITCH

There were two sisters who lived at home with their father and mother. And it so happened that the father fell sick and was not able to work. So there they were, without much money, and getting poorer every day. One sister moaned and wept and grumbled, but the other sister said, "Well, if father can't work, I can. I will go into serivce, and all the money I earn I will send home."

So she packed up some clothes in a bundle, kissed her father and mother, said good-bye to her grumpy sister, and set off for the town.

She called at this house and that house, but no one wanted a servant, so she walked on into the country. And she came to a place where there was an oven. The oven was hot, and it was full of loaves.

And the loaves called out of the oven, "Little girl, little girl, take us out, take us out! We have been baking for seven years, and no one has come to take us out."

So the girl took out the loaves, laid them on the ground, and went on her way.

She hadn't gone far when she came to a cow standing by itself in a field, with a lot of milk pails round it. And the cow said, "Little girl, little girl, milk me, milk me! Seven years I have been waiting here, and no one has come to milk me."

So the girl milked the cow into the pails. Being thirsty, she drank some of the milk, and the rest she left in the pails.

She went on a little farther and she came to an apple tree. The branches of the apple tree were so loaded with fruit that they were bowed to the ground. And the apple tree said, "Little girl, little girl, shake me, shake me! Seven years have I waited for someone to shake down my fruit, and my branches are so heavy that they will surely break!"

"You poor tree, of course I will shake you," said the girl. And she shook all the apples off the tree, propped up its branches, and left the apples in a heap on the ground.

She went a little farther and came to a house. She tapped at the door and a witch opened it. The girl asked if she wanted a servant, and the witch said she did, and that if the girl pleased her, and did what she was told, she would pay her good wages.

So the girl took service with the witch. The witch said, "Sweep and dust, cook and wash, and be careful to keep the hearth-stones clean, for as you see they are made of marble and very precious. But one thing you must never do. You must never look up the chimney, or you will repent it."

The girl worked hard, and she worked well. The witch was pleased with her; but she didn't pay the girl any wages. "If I do," thought she, "the girl will take them and go home, and I shall lose her."

Well, all went on smoothly and dully for a time. And then, one day when the witch was out, and the girl was on her knees cleaning the hearth, she forgot what the witch had said, and she looked up the chimney.

Mercy me! *Chink, chink, clitter, clatter*—a great bag full of money came tumbling down.

The girl looked up the chimney again. She looked up many times, and every time—down fell a bag of money.

"Oh!" thought the girl, "this money will keep them in comfort at home for years and years!" And she gathered up as many bags as she could carry and ran out to go home.

When she had gone some way, she heard the witch coming after her and shrieking at her to stop. So she ran to the apple tree, and said:

> "*Apple tree, apple tree, hide me,*
> *So the old witch can't find me;*
> *If she does, she'll pick my bones,*
> *And bury me under the marble stones.*"

And the apple tree said, "Climb up among my branches, and I will bend them over you."

The girl climbed up, and the apple tree criss-crossed its branches over her so that she was completely hidden.

By and by up came the witch and said:

> *"Tree of mine, tree of mine,*
>> *Have you seen a girl*
>> *With a willy-willy wag, and a long-tailed bag,*
>> *Who's stolen my money, all I had?"*

And the apple tree answered, "No, mother; not for seven years."

So the witch went off another way. And the girl climbed down from the apple tree and ran on. Just as she got to the place where the cow was grazing, she heard the witch coming after her again. So she ran to the cow, and said:

> *"Cow, cow, hide me,*
> *So the old witch can't find me;*
> *If she does, she'll pick my bones,*
> *And bury me under the marble stones."*

And the cow said, "Get behind the milk pails."

The girl crouched down behind the milk pails; and the cow gave the pails a kick, and tumbled them on top of her. Up came the witch, and said:

> *"Cow of mine, cow of mine,*
> *Have you seen a girl,*
> *With a willy-willy wag, and a long-tailed bag,*
> *Who's stolen my money, all I had?"*

And the cow answered, "No, mother; not for seven years."

So the witch turned off on another path, and the girl came out from under the milk pails, and ran on. She had got as far as the place where the oven was, when she heard the witch coming after her again. So she said:

> *"Oven, oven, hide me,*
> *So the old witch can't find me;*
> *If she does, she'll break my bones,*
> *And bury me under the marble stones."*

The girl thought to creep into the oven, but the oven said, "No, no! There's the baker, go and ask him."

So the girl ran to the baker, and he hid her under a pile of firewood.

When the witch came up, she was looking, here, there, and everywhere. She saw the baker standing by the oven, and said:

> *"Man of mine, man of mine,*
>
> *Have you seen a girl,*
>
> *With a willy-willy wag, and a long-tailed bag,*
>
> *Who's stolen my money, all I had?"*

And the baker said, "Look in the oven."

The witch went to look in the oven, and the oven said, "Get in, and look in the farthest corner." So the witch got in, and the oven slammed its door, and kept the witch inside for so long that the girl was able to get safely home.

My word—weren't there rejoicings in her home over those bags of money the girl had brought with her! The family were able now to live in comfort. The father got well again, the girl and her sister had pretty clothes to wear, and all went merrily. But the girl's sister wasn't content. She wanted more money and more money. She thought she would go into service with the witch, and get some money bags for herself.

So off she went. And when she came to the oven there it was, full of loaves again. And the loaves called to her, "Little girl, little girl, take us out, take us out! Seven years we have been baking, and no one has come to take us out."

But the girl answered, "No, I don't want to burn my fingers," and she walked on. She came to the cow, and the cow called to her, "Little girl, little girl, do milk me! Seven years I have been waiting, and no one has come to milk me."

But the girl answered, "No, I can't stop to milk you. I'm in a hurry."

She went on, and came to the apple tree. The branches of the apple tree were so loaded with fruit that they were bowed to the ground. And the apple tree called out, "Little girl, little girl, shake me, do! Seven years I have been waiting, and now my branches are so heavy that they will surely break."

The girl answered, "No, I can't stop. Another day, perhaps." And she hurried on and came to the witch's house.

The witch took her into service, and said to her, as she had said to her sister, "Sweep and dust, cook and wash, and be careful to keep the hearth-stones clean, for as you see they are made of marble and very precious. But one thing you must never do. You must never look up the chimney, or you will repent it."

The girl laughed to herself, and thought, "We'll see who repents it—you or I!"

And the very first time the witch went out the girl looked up the chimney.

Chink, chink, clitter, clatter—down fell a bag of money. The girl looked up the chimney many times; and each time—*chink, chink,* down plumped a bag of money. The girl gathered up as many bags as she could carry, and then ran out to go home. She had got as far as the apple tree, when she heard the witch coming screeching after her, so she said:

> *"Apple tree, apple tree, hide me,*
> *So the old witch can't find me'*
> *If she does, she'll break my bones,*
> *And bury me under the marble stones."*

But the apple tree said, "How can I hide you? My branches are trailing on the ground. They will break if you touch them."

So the girl ran on.

Very soon the witch came up, and said:

> *"Tree of mine, tree of mine,*
> *Have you seen a girl,*
> *With a willy-willy wag, and a long-tailed bag,*
> *Who's stolen my money, all I had?"*

And the apple tree answered, "Yes, mother; she's gone down that way."

So the witch ran, and the girl ran, but the witch ran fastest. Very soon she caught the girl, took all the money away from her, beat her soundly, and sent her home.

So all that girl carried home with her was an aching back.

Anna Wahlenberg

PETER AND THE WITCH OF THE WOOD

In a little gray hut, at the edge of a wood, lived Mother Stine and her boy who was called Peter. Mother Stine got up every morning at four o'clock and cut birch twigs and made brooms, which she sold in the city.

But Peter lay in his bed until seven, and when he arose wandered about the wood the whole day, except, of course, when he came home to eat the meal for which his mother had drudged and slaved to provide him. Yet he could well have earned his own bread, for he was a tall youth of seventeen, and big and strong and capable.

But he was an odd sort of fellow; and when he looked at himself in the dim little mirror that lay upon the chest of drawers, he felt it was really a sin that so goodlooking a chap should spoil his beauty and his fine hands with working in field and meadow.

Therefore he didn't attempt it, but set about hoping that something wonderful might happen to him. He had heard from the old gamekeeper, whom he had met upon his wanderings, that once in a while remarkable happenings occurred in that neighborhood.

The gamekeeper had even warned him with uplifted finger, and said, "Look out, Peter—look out always for the witch of the wood."

But at the same time he told Peter many things about her which were altogether tempting. Young men, especially fine-looking and attractive ones like Peter—and with a twinkle in the eye— had met with the witch of the wood, both in his father's and his grandfather's time. The witch was well disposed toward such youths who roamed about in the wood and did nothing worthwhile; and if she could get power over them and make them commit some evil or other, she would later on help them to attain honor and riches in the world.

There was, however, one small penalty attached: it could be known when they had done some evil thing. They could no longer look up frankly. But that did not matter so much, after all, for they could wear blue spectacles.

So Peter dwelt on what the gamekeeper had said, and wondered how he could manage to see the witch of the wood! And he thought long upon how to get honor and riches by committing only some small crime. One could easily do good again when one had attained to power and happiness.

"What does the witch of the wood look like?" he asked the gamekeeper one day when they met in the forest.

The old man's face wore a queer look as he answered, "She appears different to different people. Some say she is fair as the day, and others that she is ugly as sin. It seems she can assume any shape with which to dazzle one's eyes."

"I should think it would be rather amusing to meet her," said Peter.

"But I think it would be still more amusing if you went and did some work, so your mother would not have to wear herself out to find bread for two," said the gamekeeper, and then he went on his way. He could not put up with such great loafers who let other people feed and clothe them.

Peter looked angrily after him. What business was it of his or of anyone's how he lived his life, or what he did or did not do?

And, furthermore, his mother did not complain about him. She had, of course, observed with pleasure that he did not do any work; she understood perfectly well that so imposing and handsome a fellow as he could not be expected to do it. And, finally, she had moaned enough over what would happen when she was no longer able to slave and wear herself out, although the last time she had been rather more quiet about it.

Year after year she had skimped and saved, never treating herself to a bit of butter at meals, and never buying any new clothes, until at last she had saved for herself a large silver coin. And she skimped and saved through other years until the silver piece had turned into a little gold piece; and now in this present year the gold piece was so great it was equal to a whole handful of silver money.

She wore it on her breast both night and day, in a little leather bag, so no one should steal it from her; it was her joy and comfort—the dearest thing she owned after Peter, for it would help her, she said, when she could no longer see the way to help herself. If she were ill, there would be something to fall back upon; if she died, it would give her a decent burial, and Peter would have spending money when he was obliged to go out into the wide world. She was well content with the thought of her treasure, but drudged and slaved on.

"No, with Mother there is no need for all this," thought Peter; and he now wished more than ever that something lucky might befall him, when things would be still better for her.

But the luck he talked about let him wait a long time; and no matter how eagerly he sought after the witch of the wood, in crevices of mountains or behind the trunks of trees, she would not show herself.

Then it happened one evening, about the time the sun was sinking back of the treetops and he was on his way home, that he heard a strange sound. From a thicket of bushes by the road there came a deep sob.

"Who is it?" he called. At first everything was still; but soon another sob was heard, as though it came from some grief-stricken woman.

Peter pushed aside the branches, and then his eyes discovered a woman's form, seated upon a tree stump in the midst of the thicket. And she was so wonderful to look upon that his very heart began to throb. It might easily, he thought, prove to be the witch of the wood.

She was attired in a green-gold garment that fell lightly about her graceful, slender figure, while from the skirt's pleats and folds peeped out vine branches and clusters of flowers, as though they grew from the clothing itself. Her black hair, waving softly about her, was half concealed by a thin gold veil, which was wrapped about her head and hung down over breast and shoulders. But her pretty white arms were bare, and these she reached out to Peter who, hesitating and half-frightened, drew back.

"It is well you have come at last," she said, rising at the same time. Supple as a lizard, she glided through the opening in the thicket and stood before him on the road, her bright black eyes gleaming at him through the veil.

"Year in and year out I have waited for you," said she. "I have stood back of trees when you went by, I have swung in the branches over your head. But you never noticed me—and today for the first time you have heard my sobs."

"Why are you weeping?" asked Peter, still cautiously keeping his distance.

"Look." And she raised her left arm on which was a bracelet representing a snake with golden scales and green eyes; and Peter saw that from the serpent's neck hung an almost invisible chain, thin as a thread, which lost itself in the ground where she had been sitting.

When she saw his astonished glance, she pulled the chain up more and more into her hand, and then let it fall in greater and greater circles at her feet. But for all that it looked as though it would never come to an end.

"Farther than the chain reaches I cannot go," said she. "The witch of the woods holds the other end in her hand, where she sits by the spring back of the mountain's crest."

"Are you not yourself the witch of the wood?" asked Peter.

"No," she answered, and then shook her head sorrowfully. "I am a princess from a kingdom far from here. The witch of the wood stole me when I was only a little girl and took me away with her, and since then I have been her prisoner. And she has drawn the enchanted veil so tightly over my head that I cannot get it off, for she is afraid someone might get the chance to see how pretty I am—and perhaps feel so kindly toward me that he would set me free."

The poor little princess! He now understood why she sobbed, and why at this present moment she was sobbing more bitterly than before. She must be very pretty, from the glimpse he could catch through the veil. But indeed he would help her whether she was pretty or ugly. And therewith he straightened himself up, extended the muscles of his arms, and gave a quick, strong tug at the chain in his effort to break it.

But it was not so easy as he thought. The fine, thin links cut deep into his flesh but would not break. And the princess actually laughed a little at him—almost as though she considered him a fool for having attempted anything so impossible.

It made him furious. "Only just let me find the witch of the wood," he said, "and I will pull the chain from her with such force that she will stand on her nose and turn seven somersaults!"

The princess beckoned to him and then glided in among the trees. She rather floated than went, and the train of her green-gold skirt twisted itself about like a snake over the stones and the roots of the trees.

When they had come to the brow of the mountain they descended into a valley; and there among rough stones and gleaming birches lay the spring, like a shining eye wherein the clear blue heaven was reflected.

"Now you see how it is!" said the little princess who stood upon a stone and pointed to the chain. And Peter saw she had spoken the truth. The chain went directly down into the clear spring.

"Well, if one cannot manage to break it from above, one can haul it in," he thought, and immediately took hold of it. But after much tugging he again found he must give it up. He pulled so hard he was black and blue with the effort; he pulled so hard that drops of sweat trickled from his forehead, and as he worked at the chain again and again he heard smothered laughter from the princess.

"It's of no use," she finally said. "Stoop down on your knee and look into the water, so you can see the ugly witch who stands below and holds the chain. But do not be afraid."

Peter did as she said, and dismal indeed was the sight that met him in the water. The ill-favored and sallow face of a woman grinned up at him with a mouth like an empty chasm and burning black eyes like deep dark holes. And this face was wound around with a veil which exactly matched that of the little princess; and the arm and outstretched hand which held the chain were pretty and white like hers.

Could it be her reflected image?

Involuntarily he glanced about him, but there stood the woman with the veil over her face just as before. Then he began again to tug at the chain with all his might, while the face below grinned up at

him even more fiendishly than before. But every attempt proved
useless, and at last he fell over backward from the exertion.

The princess bent over him. "Come," she whispered, and drew
him with her to an overturned tree trunk, on which they sat down.

If he really wished to help her, she said, she would tell him just
what to do, and then she began to pat and stroke his hand. It was
only necessary to provide himself with some one thing or another
that would appeal to the witch of the wood, and when he threw it
into her open mouth she would be so overcome with joy that she
would forget the chain and let it slip out of her hand.

"What is it that would especially please her?" asked Peter.

The little princess stroked his hand even more affectionately and
then asked him if there was any one thing in the world which meant
more to him than all else. And Peter did not take long to think about
it. "Yes, my mother," he answered.

"Now try to remember: does she own any precious object upon
which her whole heart hangs?"

"Yes," said Peter, "a gold piece, which she always wears upon her
breast."

"That's just the very thing! You shall take it, and throw it into the
mouth of the witch of the wood."

His mother's dear gold coin, which she was more afraid of losing
than her own life! And this was to be taken from her and thrown to
the witch of the wood!

"I'll do nothing of the sort," said he. Then the little princess put
her hands before her face and sobbed aloud. Now she would never

be free, she declared, for the witch of the wood would never loosen the chain unless she received a human being's dearest possession, stolen from that person by the one loved best. Such a gift savored of a bleeding human heart, and was the sort the witch of the wood liked best.

If Peter had been willing to get this, the little princess would then have been free, and she would have led Peter to her father the king, and he would have rewarded him so handsomely that he could have made good to his mother—a thousand times over—the loss of the miserable gold piece. But he wouldn't help her, and so all must remain as it was.

Yet more loudly the little princess sobbed, and yet more confused in his mind grew Peter. Really, when one thought it over calmly, perhaps it was stupid to let luck thus slip out of his hands by not causing his mother just a little sorrow, which would soon be forgotten. And then, also, it was a great pity about the poor little princess!

"I really do not see, after all, why I should not take the coin," he concluded upon thinking it over.

Hearing this, the princess at once stopped crying, slipped her arm through his, and began to explain how it could be done. At night, when his mother was sound asleep, he should get up and cut the string which held the bag with the gold coin.

After that it would be the easiest thing in the world to possess himself of it, sneak out, and come straight to the spring in the wood. She would wait for him, the moon would shed light for them, and when she was free they could go out into the world together and be happy.

The girl's breath felt like a puff of gentle summer wind against his cheek, and her voice was so soft and insinuating that at last he felt what she advised him to do was really best both for himself and his mother.

"All right, we'll let it go at that," said he, and gave the little princess his hand upon it.

She was so delighted that she jumped up and danced twice around the tree trunk on which they had been sitting. Then she straightway followed him to the border of the wood, and when they parted she promised to come and wake him in the night by knocking on the windowpane.

So far but no farther stretched her chain.

When Peter reached home he found his mother in bed. The old woman had been up so early, in the cold morning air, and then had stood so long in the drafty market place, that when she came home she was shaking with the cold in her thin clothes. And now she was ill. She could scarcely move—only lay and moaned.

All this came at a most dreadfully inconvenient time! It was not a pleasant thing to be forced to do what had been planned, now that his mother was ill. And so he decided to put the matter off until another day. He made up the bed for his mother as well as he could, and then went to his own rest.

But in the night he was aroused by a knock on the windowpane close by his bed, and when he raised his head he saw that the moonlight flowed like a broad stream into his room, and that the little princess stood outside in her shining golden veil.

Peter opened the window. "Mother, alas, is ill, so we must wait until another time," said he.

"Another time is no time," she answered. "Your mother might die, and then the coin would no longer be worth anything. It must be taken from a living person, and not a dead one."

"Oh, no, no, I cannot do it," sobbed Peter, who had suddenly realized how good and kind his mother had always been to him.

Then the girl stamped on the ground with anger. If he would not do at once what he had promised she would go away and never come back, for there was no difficulty in getting hold of that coin. If his mother should wake, all he need say was that he had to have it to buy medicine for her.

With this she gave him a push, and Peter felt there was nothing more to do but go to his mother's bed, take the penknife from his pocket, and feel around after the cord upon the invalid's neck. He got hold of this cord, but when he went to cut it his mother turned over in bed.

"Is that you up again, and straightening the covers for me, my boy?" she said. "How good and kind you are to your sick mother."

At that moment he felt that the cord, from which the coin hung, was loose, but he could not find out where the gold piece had slipped.

So Peter was obliged to tell his mother that it was necessary to have money with which to buy medicine.

"Medicine? No, most certainly not. The gold coin will be needed for a coffin, and for spending money for my Peter when he shall go out into the wide world." And with that she pressed her treasure close to her breast and, though she writhed with pain, held onto it stubbornly with her wrinkled fingers, and finally she slept, without the treasure slipping from her grasp.

Then Peter heard his name whispered from the open window, and there the girl stood again, with her arms upon the sill. She held out to him between her two fingers a small flat stone.

"Now you can pull out the bag," she said when Peter came to her, "take the gold piece from it, and lay in its stead this stone, which is so much of the same size that your mother will notice nothing."

Peter paused. He felt there was something hideous in the very suggestion, but the princess began again on how happy they would be when he had secured the gold piece and she was free. So Peter thought over the matter for the second time.

Then softly he crept back to his mother's bed and cautiously felt around for the bag, which he soon found, for sleep had let it slip from the wrinkled fingers. The next moment the coin was replaced by the flat stone, and the bag lay again upon his mother's breast.

Once more she awoke, and gazed upon him. "My own dear boy," she said, "I feel I am going to die, and as I lay here I have thought it best you should take my gold piece first as last. But buy no expensive coffin for me, Peter, only a neat one, with a little white pillow in it. You will have more need of the money yourself when you go out into the world."

With that she held out the bag to Peter. But Peter felt as though he could not move.

"Take it, nevertheless, Peter, take it," persisted his mother. "And when the gold piece is gone, still keep the bag; and when you look upon it remember your old mother, who always thought about you whenever she put anything in it. Take it now, Peter, and come and kiss me."

Peter bent down quickly and took the bag from her hand; but instead of kissing her he went to the window where the girl stood and beckoned him. He was overcome with shame for what he had done, and when he saw the eager outstretched fingers a great anger seized him.

"You shall have this, since you would delude me into cheating my own mother," he hissed between his teeth. And at the same moment he flung the bag in the girl's face.

Her veil was torn by the stone, and through the rent could be seen an ugly sallow face with a yawning cavern for a mouth and two black holes for eyes—exactly like the face he had seen in the spring behind the mountain's crest.

It was indeed the witch of the wood; and it was she who had let herself be mirrored in the water—being quick enough to deceive him as she pulled her veil up and down.

Scarcely had he realized this before she, snorting and foaming like some wild creature, threw herself at him as though to grab him in her arms. But the chain was too short. She could not reach him. And when Peter took up a pail of water and threw it all over her, she turned away and then vanished like a gray mist.

"It must be frightful weather tonight," said Peter's mother, to whom all this performance had sounded like hail and storm.

But Peter made a new bag for the gold piece, and hung it about his mother's neck.

"You shall have your coin again, Mother," said he, "for it cannot be the truth that you are to die now. I shall nurse you, and hereafter I shall work for you, and you shall have it easy all the rest of your life."

Then the old woman began to cry for joy, because she had never heard Peter talk like this before, and out of pure curiosity to see if afterward he would keep his word, she was actually better the next day!

And to her joy he did what he had promised. At the time the reapers were in the field the following morning, he had slung his scythe over his shoulder and had gone to compete with the men in the town. Never any more did his mother have to stand in the market place and sell brooms. They certainly were not rich, but they did well; and the next time Peter met the gamekeeper he was patted kindly by him on the shoulder.

"You have certainly got good eyes, Peter," said he. "At one time it looked as though you would soon have to wear blue spectacles. But now your glance is open and frank, and there is an air of contentment about you."

The witch of the wood hardly felt the same way. Because, no matter how often Peter went through the wood, he never saw so much as the hem of her green-gold gown.

OLD SPELLS AND CHARMS
Traditional English Rhymes

A Witch's Spell

I went to the toad that lies under the wall,

I charmed him out, and he came at my call;

I scratched out the eyes of the owl before,

I tore the bat's wing: what would you have more?

Old Counting Rhyme

Hinx, minx, the old witch winks,

The fat begins to fry,

Nobody at home but jumping Joan,

Father, mother, and I!

Halloween Spell

To be recited as a chestnut is
thrown into the fire on Halloween.

If you love me, pop and fly,

If you hate me, lay and die.

Charm to Protect Against Witches

Matthew, Mark, Luke and John

Bless the bed that I lie on.

Four corners to my bed,

Five angels there lie spread

Two at my head and two at my feet

And one at my heart my soul to keep.

Eleanore M. Jewett

WHICH WAS WITCH?

There was once a wise and learned man named Kim Su-ik. He lived just inside the south gate of Seoul but he might as well have lived anywhere for all the thought he gave the matter. His mind was entirely taken up with study and books, and one could say of him, as Im Bang said of another scholar, "He used to awake at first cockcrow, wash, dress, take his book and never lay it aside. On his right were pictures, on his left were books, and he happy between. He rose to be a Prime Minister."

One night Kim Su-ik was absorbed in studying a Chinese classic when he suddenly felt hungry. He clapped his hands to summon a servant, and immediately the door of his room opened.

His wife stepped in.

"What does the master of the house desire?" said she.

"Food," he answered briefly, his attention already returned to the book in his lap.

"I have little in the house but a few roasted chestnuts. If that will suffice I will bring them to you myself. The servants have long since gone to their sleeping quarters."

Kim Su-ik grunted his approval and went on with his studies. In a very short time the door opened again and his wife came in bearing a brass bowl full of hot roasted chestnuts. He helped himself to one and was in the act of putting it into his mouth when once more the door opened and in stepped his wife with a brass bowl of hot roasted chestnuts.

But his wife was already there, standing beside him with the bowl in her hands!

Kim Su-ik, his mouth still open and a chestnut half in it, looked in astonishment from one to the other of the identical women. They were as like as two pins—faces, features, figures, clothes, the way they stood, the way they used their fingers and moved their shoulders. Never were twins more completely alike. Kim Su-ik passed his hands before his eyes. He must have overdone his studying, he thought to himself, read too late and too steadily. His eyes were playing tricks on him, that was all. He was seeing double.

But when he looked again the two women were still there, and what was stranger still, they seemed not to be aware of each other, but stood quietly, gracefully, their eyes fastened on him as if waiting to know his pleasure.

The scholar leaped to his feet, choking back the cry of terror that rose in his throat. He knew, suddenly, without a doubt, what this meant. It was midnight, the moon was at the full, ghosts, evil spirits, witches and goblins would be abroad, filled with power. One of these two creatures standing before him was his wife, known and loved by him all his wedded life—and perhaps not quite fully appreciated, he hastily decided. The other must be a witch, able to change into any form she chose in the twinkling of an eye. But *which was which?* How could he protect his wife and drive this evil double from beside her?

Being a quick thinker as well as a learned one, Kim Su-ik plunged into action. He seized the arm of one of the women with his right hand and before the other could realize what he was about, he had her arm fast in his left hand. They turned mildly reproachful eyes upon him but made no effort to free themselves.

"My dear," said one, "too much study has fevered your brain."

"My dear," said the other, "too much reading of books has affected your mind."

Kim Su-ik looked from one to the other. Not a particle of difference was there to give him a hint as to which was wife and which was witch. He shook them gently. They smiled indulgently as at a child. He shook harder. No resentment, no struggle to get free. He was tempted to relax his grip on the two arms, but he knew he must not for a moment do that, and hung on more firmly than ever.

Minutes went by, then hours, the dull slow moving hours between midnight and cockcrow. Three stood silent, motionless, in the same spot. Kim Su-ik grew weary beyond words. So, too, must his wife be weary, but neither of the two women he held so tightly by the arm said anything or showed by any movement or expression of the face that she was tired, puzzled or angry. His wife would have been tired and puzzled—angry, too, perhaps, but she would not have blustered or scolded. Any other woman would, were she witch or human. But surely his wife would say *something*. What in the world had got into her? Was she bewitched? Or walking in her sleep? Perhaps she was not either one of these two women. He wanted to rush into the other part of the house to see if she was there, thus providing that both of these were witches. But he did nothing, just hung on, grimly, silently.

At long last a cock crowed. Immediately the woman at his left tried to wrench her arm free. The other remained quiet. Kim Su-ik dropped the unresisting one and threw all his strength into a struggle with the other. Like a wild thing the creature fought, biting, snarling, spitting, leaping back and forth. Still the scholar held on to her and would not let go. The arm in his hand shrank and grew hairy. The whole figure dwindled, the eyes grew round and green and blazed with fury.

Another cock crowed and another, and the first gray light of dawn melted the dark shadows out of doors. But Kin Su-ik had no thought or time to notice the coming of day. With a hideous shriek the creature changed before his very eyes into a powerful wildcat. In horror he loosed his hold, and she leaped through the window and was gone.

"I still think you are studying too much," said a quiet, familiar voice behind him, and there stood his wife, pale, trembling a little, but smiling confidently.

"Why didn't you let me know which was which?" demanded Kim Su-ik.

His wife laughed. "I don't know what you are talking about! You behaved very strangely, but then, one never knows what to expect of a scholar. Which was which what?"

"Witch!" said Kim Su-ik.

Ruth Manning-Sanders

LAZY HANS

Now you must know that there was a widow who had a lazy son. Hans was his name. That lad wouldn't stir a finger to help his mother; he sat in the sun all day, and expected her to feed and clothe him.

Well, when he was a little chap, that was all right; but when he grew into a great strong hulk of a fellow, his mother could stand his ways no longer.

So one day she took a stick to him and said, "Be off! Earn your own bread and trouble me no more!"

"Oh, all right, if that's how you feel," said Hans.

And he got up from the grass where he was lying, and leisurely took the road.

He ambled along the road, and he ambled along the road. When he saw nuts in the hedge, he picked and ate them; and when he saw a bright stream at his side, he cupped his hands and drank. When he came to a soft place of moss and fallen leaves, he laid him down and slept.

Thought he, "What is all this chatter about work? A fellow can live quite well without it!"

All right; so he could, for a bit. But then he came into a barren country—a country where no hedges grew, where no streams flowed, where the pools were brackish, and the ground was covered with prickles.

Thought he, "I have only to walk on a little farther, and I shall find something different."

So he walked a little farther, but he didn't find anything different, except that the country became more barren, and yet more barren. And he was hungry and thirsty and desolate-feeling.

Then he came to a little straggly wood, and all the leaves had fallen from the trees and were lying about in yellow withered heaps. He walked through the wood, and a bit of a way farther on was a small stone house, with a great barn at the side of it.

Said he to himself, "Perhaps whoever lives here will give me something to eat." And he went and knocked at the door.

Out came an old witch. She squinted at him and said, "What do you want?"

"Something to eat," said Hans.

"Something to eat, indeed!" said she. "If you want something to eat you must work for it."

"Oh, all right, if that's how you feel, I will work."

"Mind you, it will be easy work," said the witch.

"The easier the better," said Hans.

So she took him in, and gave him a plate of bread and cheese, and some water to drink. "Now you can go and sleep in the barn," said she. "You will start work at dawn tomorrow."

"Isn't that a bit too early?" said Hans.

"No," snapped the witch, "it is not too early. Go to the barn."

"I would rather sleep by the fire," said Hans.

"You will sleep in the barn," said the witch. And she drove him out and bolted the door against him.

There was nothing whatever in the barn. It had a stone floor, and was cold and draughty. There wasn't even a sack or a truss of straw to make Hans a bed. He had a restless night of it, but he fell asleep at last, and woke stiff and cold to find the witch shaking him.

"Surely it's not dawn yet!" he said.

"Dawn indeed!" snapped the witch. "The sun has risen!"

And, sure enough, when Hans came out of the barn, yawning and rubbing his eyes, a pale ghost of a sun was peering at him over the top of the straggly wood.

He got bread for his breakfast, and a mug of cold water. He asked for cheese, but the witch wouldn't give him any. "Cheese is for supper when you've done your work," she said.

Said Hans, "You needn't snap my head off."

Said she, "I'll twist your neck round three times if you don't mind your manners!"

"I think I'll be going," said Hans.

"You'll not be going till you've earned your night's lodging," said she. And she laid a spell on the threshold so that Hans couldn't cross it.

"Well then," said he, "tell me what I must do. You said it was to be easy work; and if it isn't easy work, you won't find me doing it."

The witch gave him a heavy stick, as big as himself, and pointed at one end.

"And what am I to do with this?" said Hans.

Said she, "Three miles from here, if you walk westward, you will come to a field of corn. What you have to do is to plant the stick in the middle of the cornfield."

"Is that all?" said Hans.

"That's all," said she.

"Oh ho!" said he, "I'll soon do that!"

"The sooner the better," said the witch.

So Hans set out with the stick. He went westward, and the way led him back through the straggly wood. The stick was heavy, and he was feeling stiff and sleepy after his restless night. So, in the middle of the wood he sat down on a heap of yellow leaves.

"There's no hurry. It can't take me all day to walk three miles and back," he thought. "So I'll just have a nap before I go on."

He sat on that pile of leaves, yawning and yawning, and soon he fell asleep. When he woke up it was evening. "Oh lord!" thought he, "if I have to walk three miles to that field and three miles back again, I shall be benighted. I won't do it! What's the sense, anyway, of planting a stick in the middle of a cornfield? The old woman's crazy!

One place to plant a stick is as good as another—it won't grow wherever it's planted."

So what did he do but push the point of the stick into a pile of leaves. And he left it standing there, and sauntered back to the witch's house.

"Did you plant the stick as I told you?" said she.

"I did," said Hans.

"You've taken your time about it," said she.

"Well, and why not?" said Hans.

She gave him his supper of bread and cheese.

"But I'm not going to bed in that barn again unless you give me something to lie on," said Hans.

"There'll be plenty to lie on by the morning," said the witch.

"I'm not talking of the morning, I'm talking of now," said Hans.

The witch threw him a bundle of sacks; and he took them, went to the barn, rolled himself up in the sacks, and fell asleep. At midnight he was wakened by a rattling at the door that sounded like hail. He went to the door to look out, but it flew open before he reached it, and a cloud of yellow leaves whirled in and hit him in the face.

"Welcome!" said Hans, "however you've got here! You'll make me a good, soft bed." And he beat the leaves off with his hands, and began piling them up in a corner. But *swish, hurry, scurry*—in whirled more leaves, and more and more, and they came with such headlong speed that they knocked him backwards. They were up to his knees now, and they were spinning round his head, and hitting him in the face and blinding him.

Hans struggled his way to the door to try and shut it, but the door wouldn't shut, and still a thick cloud of leaves was whirling in from outside. He put his head down and fought his way through them. And when he got through them, what did he see by the light of a waning moon? He saw the witch's stick hopping along on its pointed end, and driving the leaves before it.

When the barn was full to the roof, the stick hopped its way back into the witch's house, and Hans sat down on the doorstep to wait till morning.

At sunrise the witch came out. She was nodding her head and smiling from ear to ear. "So the barn's full!" she said.

"Full to the roof," said Hans.

"Then we shan't starve next winter," said the witch.

She went to the barn and flung open the door. She gave a shriek. "Leaves!" she screamed, "*Leaves!* What's the meaning of this? Where's the corn? Didn't you plant the stick in the cornfield?"

"I did not," said Hans. "I fell asleep in the wood, and when I woke up it was dark. So I planted the stick in the wood and came back. How was I to know what the stick would do?"

"You lazy pig!" screamed the witch.

"You needn't call me names," said Hans.

"It's more than names, it's facts!" she shouted.

And she whipped a large iron ring out of her pocket and tossed it into Hans' face.

What Hans had been going to say, I can't tell you; for all he did say was *"Grumph!"* She had turned him into a pig.

"Since you're so fond of the wood you can go and live in it!" she said. "And when I've fattened you up, I'll eat you."

Pig-Hans ran off to the wood. He didn't mean to stay there. He didn't like the idea of being eaten. So he thought he would get out on the far side of the wood and go home. But the witch laid a spell all round the trees, and he couldn't get beyond them. So in the wood he had to stay.

Every morning and every evening the witch came to the wood with a pail of swill for him. But though Hans felt very hungry he scarcely ate any of it. He was too afraid of getting fat and fit to eat. But what Hans left of the swill, and that was most of it, the foxes came and ate up, so that the pail was always empty when the witch came for it.

"Get fat, get fat, get fat!" screamed the witch, poking and pinching him. "Why don't you get fat?"

But Pig-Hans got thinner and thinner. And at last the witch said, "Well, if I can't fatten you, I may as well take you for a servant again." And she pulled the ring out of the pig's nose and turned Hans back into a man.

"Are you going to work for me and obey orders now?" said the witch.

Said Hans, "If I must, I suppose I must."

"See you do," said the witch. And she fetched her stick and told him to go and plant it in a dairy ten miles away, so that it might bring all the milk churns into the barn.

Hans set out. He meant to go and plant the stick where he was told this time. He walked valiantly for five miles, and he walked less valiantly for another three miles; and it seemed to him that the stick got heavier and heavier. He walked on for another mile, but he could scarcely drag one foot behind the other. "I must just have five minutes rest," he said to himself. And seeing a large mound by the wayside, he clambered up on to it, thrust the stick upright into the middle of it, lay down, and was soon fast asleep.

When he woke up it was dark. He scrambled to his feet, and felt about for the stick. Well, well, for a long time he couldn't find it anywhere. It had sunk deep down, and there was not more than half an inch of the head of it standing up above the mound. When at last Hans' groping fingers found this half inch, he tried to pull the stick out. But it was wedged tight between two hard pieces of metal, and he couldn't budge it.

He gave up trying at last, and decided to walk away and away into the night, and never go back to the witch's house. And he did walk away, but the witch had put a spell on the road; and the way he had come was the way he must walk back, however much he tried to walk in the opposite direction.

So there he was at last back in the barn; and as before, he was wakened at midnight by a rattling at the door. The door flew open but it wasn't milk churns that the stick was driving in: it was tin cans and pieces of cart wheels, and broken glass and china, and rusty pots and leaky kettles, and bits of bedsteads; for the mound where he had left the stick was an old rubbish dump.

Hans was cut and bruised and battered and scared out of his wits, before he could make his way out through all this rubbish. And still it came pouring in. And behind the rubbish came the stick, hopping along on its pointed end, driving the rubbish before it.

When the barn was full to the roof, the stick hopped its way back into the witch's house, and Hans sat down on the doorstep to wait till morning.

At sunrise the witch came out, nodding her head and smiling from ear to ear.

"Did you go to sleep in the wood again?" said she.

"I did not," said Hans.

"Did you plant the stick as I told you?"

"I did," said Hans.

"And is the barn full?"

"Full to the roof," said Hans.

"Ah ha!" said the witch, "then we shall have plenty of milk!"

She went to the barn, and flung open the door. But when she saw all the rubbish piled up to the roof, she screamed with rage.

"Well," said Hans, "I couldn't help it. I feel asleep on the mound and put the stick to stand behind my head. It sank in, and I couldn't pull it out. *I'm* not to blame for the antics it plays."

"You've no more sense than a gander!" screamed the witch.

"You needn't . . . " began Hans. But whatever he meant to say, all he did was to hiss. For the witch had tied a striped scarf round his neck, and turned him into a gander.

"And don't think starving yourself will do you any good this time," she yelled, "for fat or thin, I'll cook you for Christmas!"

Gander-Hans hissed again; he stretched out his neck and pecked at the witch's feet. She gave a jump back and he gave a run in the opposite direction; the witch hadn't had time to put a spell around the house, so Gander-Hans spread his wings and flew away.

He flew and flew and flew until he came to a wide meadow, where a flock of geese were nibbling at the grass. Then he furled his wings and came down.

"Oh look!" cried the geese, "look at this queer gander with a scarf round his neck!"

"It's a decoration," said Gander-Hans, who found he could speak goose-language quite well. "It was tied round my neck by a queen. No other gander in the world has a decoration like mine!" And he began to waddle about and stretch out his neck. "You see how the colours glitter when the sun catches them."

"What did you do to win it?" asked the geese, who were very impressed.

"I brought her all sorts of valuable things," said Gander-Hans. "Things she couldn't possibly have obtained otherwise. I went through great perils and dangers to procure them. Oh, I can tell you, I didn't get this decoration for nothing! And now that I have come among you, I expect to be treated with due respect."

The geese did treat him with respect. In fact, they squabbled as to which of them should feed nearest to him, and he teased them by favouring first one and then another. He nibbled the meadow grass and it tasted good to him; and when he was tired of nibbling the grass, he spread his great white wings and flew to bathe in a nearby lake; and all the geese spread their wings and came after him, pecking, and hissing and trying to jostle each other away from his side.

"Ha! Ha! Ha!" laughed Gander-Hans. "This is a fine life. Plenty to eat, plenty to drink, plenty of admiration—and no work!"

And he lived with the geese for a whole year.

But one day in spring there was a clanging of wings in the air, and a big white bird came flying over the meadow. Another gander! The new gander circled once or twice over the meadow, and then down he swooped and alighted on the grass in the midst of the geese.

"Get out!" hissed Gander-Hans.

"Get out yourself," hissed the new gander. "You with a rag around your neck!"

"A decoration, you mean!" said Gander-Hans.

"I said a rag, and I mean a rag," said the new gander. And he gave a peck at the scarf.

Now to tell the truth the scarf was no longer bright and gay, for it had been bleached by the sun, and frayed by the wind, and soaked so often by the water of the lake that it did indeed look more like a rag than anything else. But Gander-Hans reminded himself that he was really a man and not a bird, and he wasn't going to stand any cheek from a mere gander. So he gave that mere gander a vicious peck; and next minute they were at it, hammer and tongs, with feathers flying, and bills snapping, and the geese standing round in an admiring circle to watch the combat.

Which one of those ganders would have defeated the other, there is no telling; for in the struggle the new gander got his bill firmly wedged in the frayed knot of Gander-Hans' scarf; the knot came undone, the scarf fell off, Gander-Hans immediately vanished, and in his place stood Hans.

The new gander stretched out his neck and hissed. Hans raised his arm and shouted, "Be off!" The new gander waddled away sideways, stretching his neck out, turning his head over his shoulder, and hissing as he went. The geese followed him. They also were hissing; and suddenly the whole flock rose into the air, and flew away.

"Well—I'll be—blowed!" said Hans.

He lifted his arms, he looked at his hands, he felt his face, he bent his knees, he examined one foot and then the other foot. A man again—and what next? No good now to fill his stomach with grass; no good now to go and float on the water. "I think I had better go home," he said to himself.

But where was home?

He set off walking westward, since it was from the west he had come. After walking for some hours, he saw on the horizon to the north the straggly wood near the witch's house. "I will keep clear of that, at all events," he said to himself. But it gave him his direction, and he came at last on to the fringes of the barren country where he had suffered hunger and thirst, and after that into the fertile country where he had picked nuts and drunk from pleasant streams. And there in the distance he saw the smoke rising from his mother's cottage.

Then he ran, for it came over him how pleased he was to get home, and how much better it was to be a man than a lazy pig or a senseless gander. So he opened the door of his mother's cottage, and there she was sitting by the fire.

She was secretly overjoyed to see him, for she had been feeling very lonely. But all she said was, "So you've come again, Hans!"

"Yes, Mother, I've come again. You may not believe it, but I've been a pig, and I've geen a gander. And I find it is better to be a man."

"But a man has to work, Hans!"

"I know that, Mother. And now I will work for you."

And he did work for his mother, and kept her in comfort from that day on. So she lived happily, and he lived happily, ever after.

Charles J. Finger
THE MAGIC BALL

A cold-eyed witch lived in the Cordilleras and when the first snow commenced to fall she was always full of glee, standing on a rock, screaming like a wind-gale and rubbing her hands. For it pleased her to see the winter moon, the green country blotted out, the valleys white, the trees snow-laden, and the waters ice-bound and black. Winter has her hunting time and her eating time, and in the summer she slept. So she was full of a kind of savage joy when there were leaden clouds and drifting gales, and she waited and watched, waited and watched, ever ready to spring upon frost-stiffened creatures that went wandering down to the warmer lowlands.

This witch was a wrinkled creature, hard of eye, thin-lipped, with hands that looked like roots of trees, and so tough was her skin that knife could not cut nor arrow pierce it. In the country that swept down to the sea she was greatly feared, and hated, too. The hate came because by some strange magic she was able to draw children to her one by one, and how she did it no man knew. But the truth is that she had a magic ball, a ball bright and shining and of many colours, and this she left in places where children played, but never where man or woman could see it.

One day, near the lake called Oretta, a brother and sister were at play and saw the magic ball at the foot of a little hill. Pleased with its brightness and beauty Natalia ran to it, intending to pick it up and take it home, but, to her surprise, as she drew near to it the ball rolled away; then, a little way off, came to rest again. Again she ran to it and almost had her hand on it when it escaped, exactly as a piece of thistle-down does, just as she was about to grasp it. So she followed it, always seeming to be on the point of catching it but never doing so, and as she ran her brother Luis followed, careful lest she should come to harm. The strange part of it was that every time the ball stopped it rested close to some berry bush or by the edge of a crystal-clear spring, so that she, like all who were thus led away, always found at the moment of resting something to eat or to drink or to refresh herself. Nor, strangely enough, did she tire, but because of the magic went skipping and running and jumping just as long as she followed the ball. Nor did any one under the spell of that magic note the passing of time, for days were like hours and a night like the shadow of a swiftly flying cloud.

At last, chasing the ball, Natalia and Luis came to a place in the valley where the Rio Chico runs between great hills, and it was dark and gloomy and swept by heavy gray clouds. The land was strewn with mighty broken rocks and here and there were patches of snow, and soon great snow flakes appeared in the air. Then boy and girl were terror-struck, for they knew with all the wandering and twisting and turning they had lost their way. But the ball still rolled on, though slower now, and the children followed. But the air grew keener and colder and the sun weaker, so that they were very glad indeed when they came to a black rock where, at last, the ball stopped.

Natalia picked it up, and for a moment gazed at its beauty, but for a moment only. For no sooner had she gazed at it and opened her lips to speak than it vanished as a soap bubble does, at which her grief was great. Luis tried to cheer her and finding that her hands were icy cold led her to the north side of the rock where it was warmer, and there he found a niche like a lap between two great arms, and in the moss-grown cranny Natalia coiled herself up and was asleep in a minute. As for Luis, knowing that as soon as his sister had rested they must set out about finding a way home, he sat down intending to watch. But not very long did he keep his eyes open, for he was weary and sad at heart. He tried hard to keep awake, even holding his eyelids open with his fingers, and he stared hard at a sunlit hilltop across the valley, but even that seemed to make him sleepy. Then, too, there were slowly nodding pine trees and the whispering of leaves, coming in a faint murmur from the mountainside. So, soon, Luis slept.

Natalia, being out of the blustering wind, was very comfortable in the little niche between the great stone arms, and she dreamed that she was at home. Her mother, she thought, was combing her hair and singing as she did so. So she forgot her hunger and weariness, and in her dreamland knew nothing of the bare black rocks and snow-patched hills. Instead, she seemed to be at home where the warm firelight danced on the walls and lighted her father's brown face to a lively red as he mended his horse gear. She saw her brother, too, with his jet-black hair and cherry-red lips. But her mother, she thought, grew rough and careless and pulled her hair, so that she gave a little cry of pain and awoke. Then in a flash she knew where she was and was chilled to the bone with the piercing wind that swept down from the mountain top. Worse still, in front of her stood the old witch of the hills, pointing, pointing, pointing with knotty forefinger, and there were nails on her hands and feet that looked like claws.

Natalia tried to rise, but could not, and her heart was like stone when she found what had happened. It was this: while she slept, the witch had stroked and combed her hair, and meanwhile wrought magic, so that the girl's hair was grown into the rock so very close that she could not as much as turn her head. All that she could do was to stretch forth her arms, and when she saw Luis a little way off she called to him most piteously. But good Luis made no move. Instead, he stood with arms wide apart like one who feels a wall in the dark, moving his hands this way and that. Then Natalia wept, not understanding and little knowing that the witch had bound Luis with a spell, so that there seemed to be an invisible wall around the rock through which he could not pass, try as he would. But he heard the witch singing in her high and cracked voice, and this is what she sang:

> "Valley all pebble-sown,
> Valley where wild winds moan!
> Come, mortals, come.
>
> "Valley so cool and white,
> Valley of winter night,
> Come, children, come.
>
> "Straight like a shaft to mark,
> Come they to cold and dark,
> Children of men!"

Then she ceased and stood with her root-like finger upraised, and from near by came the voice of a great white owl, which took up the song, saying:

> "Things of the dark and things without name,
> Save us from light and the torch's red flame."

Now all this was by starlight, but the moment the owl had ceased, from over the hill came a glint of light as the pale moon rose, and with a sound like a thunderclap the witch melted into the great rock and the owl flapped away heavily.

"Brother," whispered the girl, "you heard what the owl said?"

"Yes, sister, I heard," he answered.

"Brother, come to me. I am afraid," said Natalia, and commenced to cry a little.

"Sister," he said, "I try but I cannot. There is something through which I cannot pass. I can see but I cannot press through."

"Can you not climb over, dear Luis?" asked Natalia.

"No, Natalia. I have reached high as I can, but the wall that I cannot see goes up and up."

"Is there no way to get in on the other side of the rock, dear, dear Luis? I am very cold and afraid, being here alone."

"Sister, I have walked around. I have felt high and low. But it is always the same. I cannot get through, I cannot climb over, I cannot crawl under. But I shall stay here with you, so fear not."

At that Natalia put her hands to her face and wept a little, but very quietly, and it pained Luis to see the tears roll down her cheeks and turn to little ice pearls as they fell. After a while Natalia spoke again, but through sobs.

"Brother mine, you heard what the owl said?"

"Yes, sister."

"Does it mean nothing to you?" she asked.

"Nothing," he replied.

"But listen," said Natalia. "These were the words: 'Save us from light and the torch's red flame.'"

"I heard that, Natalia. What does it mean?"

"It means, brother, that the things in this horrible valley fear fire. So go, brother. Leave me a while but find fire, coming back with it swiftly. There will be sickening loneliness, so haste, haste."

Hearing that, Luis was sad, for he was in no mood to leave his sister in that plight. Still she urged him, saying: "Speed, brother, speed."

Even then he hesitated, until with a great swoop there passed over the rock a condor wheeling low, and it said as it passed: "Fire will conquer frosted death."

"You hear, brother," said Natalia. "So speed and find fire and return before night."

Then Luis stayed no longer, but waved his sister a farewell and set off down the valley, following the condor that hovered in the air, now darting away and now returning. So Luis knew that the great bird led him, and he ran, presently finding the river and following it until he reached the great vega where the waters met.

At the meeting of the waters he came to a house, a poor thing made of earth and stones snuggled in a warm fold of the hills. No one was about there, but as the condor flew high and, circling in the air, became a small speck, Luis knew that it would be well to stay a while and see what might befall. Pushing open the door he saw by the ashes in the fireplace that someone lived there, for there were red embers well covered to keep the fire alive. So seeing that the owner of the house would return soon he made himself free of the place, which was the way of that country, and brought fresh water from the spring. Then he gathered wood and piled it neatly by the fireside. Next he blew upon the embers and added twigs and sticks until a bright fire glowed, after which he took the broom of twigs and swept the earth floor clean.

How the man of the house came into the room Luis never knew, but there he was, sitting by the fire on a stool. He looked at things but said nothing to Luis, only nodding his head. Then he brought bread and yerba and offered some to Luis. After they had eaten the old man spoke, and this is what he said:

"Wicked is the white witch, and there is but one way to defeat her. What, lad, is the manner of her defeat? Tell me that."

Then Luis, remembering what the condor had said, repeated the words: "'Fire will conquer frosted death.'"

"True," said the man slowly, nodding his head. "And your sister is there. Now here comes our friend the condor, who sees far and knows much."

> "Now with cold grows faint her breath,
>   Fire will conquer frosted death."

Having said that the great bird wheeled up sharply.

But no sooner was it out of sight than a turkey came running and stood a moment, gobbling. To it the old man gave a lighted brand, repeating the words the condor had spoken.

Off sped the turkey with the blazing stick, running through marsh and swamp in a straight line, and Luis and the old man watched. Soon the bird came to a shallow lagoon, yet made no halt. Straight through the water it sped, and so swiftly that the spray dashed up on either side. High the turkey held the stick, but not high enough, for the splashing water quenched the fire, and seeing that, the bird returned, dropping the blackened stick at the old man's feet.

"Give me another, for the maiden is quivering cold," said the turkey. "This time I will run around the lake."

"No. No," answered the man. "You must know that when the water spirit kisses the fire king, the fire king dies. So, that you may remember, from now and forever you will carry on your feathers the marks of rippling water."

Down again swooped the condor and a little behind him came a goose, flying heavily. As before, the condor cried:

"Now with cold grows faint her breath,
Fire will conquer frosted death,"

then flew away again toward the witch mountain.

To the goose the old man gave a blazing stick and at once the brave bird set off, flying straight in the direction the condor had taken. Over vega and over lagoon she went, pausing only at a snowclad hilltop, because the stick had burned close to her beak. So she dropped it in the snow to get a better hold, and when she picked it up again there was but a charred thing. Sad enough the goose returned to the house, bearing the blackened stick, and begged to be given another chance.

"No. No," said the old man. "The silver snow queen's kiss is death to the fire king. That is something you must remember. From now on and for ever you must carry feathers of gray like the ashes. But here comes the condor and we must hear his message."

Sadly then the goose went away, her feathers ash gray, and the condor wheeled low again, calling:

"Fainter grows the maiden's breath,
Night must bring the frosted death,"

and having said, like an arrow he shot off.

No sooner had he gone than the long-legged, long-billed flamingo dropped to the ground.

"Your beak is long," said the old man, "but fly swiftly, for the stick is short."

The flamingo took the burning stick by the end and made straight for the mountain, racing with all possible speed. As for Luis, he made up his mind to tarry no longer and set off, running like a deer. But an ostrich, seeing him, spread her wings like sails and ran by his side. On her back Luis placed his hand, and with that help sped as fast as the flamingo. In the air the flamingo went like an arrow, resting not, although the blazing fire burned her neck and breast until it became pink and red. But that she heeded not. Straight up the valley and to the rock where Natalia was bound went she, and into a heap of dried moss on the south side of the rock she dropped the blazing stick. Up leaped dancing flames, and with a tremendous noise the rock flew into a thousand pieces and the power of the witch was gone for ever. As for Natalia, she was at once freed, and with her gentle, cool hand stroked the breast of the flamingo so that the burns were healed, but as a sign of its bravery the bird has carried a crimson breast from that day to this.

As for Natalia and Luis, they lived for many, many years in the valley, and about them birds of many kinds played and lived and reared their young, and the magic ball of the witch lived only in the memory of men.

WITCHES' CHANT
William Shakespeare

Round about the cauldron go;
In the poisoned entrails throw.
Toad, that under cold stone
Days and nights has thirty-one
Swelt'red venom, sleeping got,
Boil thou first i' th' charméd pot.

Double, double, toil and trouble,
Fire burn and cauldron bubble.

Fillet of a fenny snake,
In the cauldron boil and bake;
Eye of newt, and toe of frog,
Wool of bat, and tongue of dog,
Adder's fork, and blindworm's sting,
Lizard's leg, and howlet's wing—
For a charm of pow'rful trouble
Like a hell-broth boil and bubble.

Double, double, toil and trouble,
Fire burn and cauldron bubble.